"Wait! Before You Say Anything, I Want To Ask You Something.

"I wondered if you'd go to a Halloween party with me," Megan asked over the phone.

"Yes," Tom replied. He was smiling. He couldn't help himself.

He heard Megan continue hesitantly, "I'll call you later with the details. Think about what costume you want to wear. Maybe we'll come up with something that matches. All right?"

"Sure, Megan," he replied calmly. They said their goodbyes. When Tom heard the phone click he scrambled out of his chair so fast it fell over backward. He stumbled over the coffee table and banged his hip on the edge of the dining room table on his way outside.

Please be there, he silently begged as he jerked the lid off the trash can. There it was. Right on top. *HOW TO MARRY THE WOMAN OF YOUR DREAMS.*

He tenderly rescued the book from its place on a pile of old newspapers and tucked it under his arm. Once he got back inside, he turned on every light in the house, settled into an armchair and opened the book....

Dear Reader:

I hope you've been enjoying 1989, our "Year of the Man" at Silhouette Desire. Every one of the twelve authors who are contributing a *Man of the Month* has created a very special someone for your reading pleasure. Each man is unique, and each author's style, plot and characterization give you a different insight into her man's story.

From January to December, 1989 will be a twelve-month extravaganza, spotlighting one book each month with special cover treatment as a tribute to the Silhouette Desire hero—our *Man of the Month*!

You'll find these men who've been created by your favorite authors irresistible. Naomi Horton's Slater McCall is indeed *A Dangerous Kind of Man*, coming this April, and love, betrayal, greed and revenge are all part of Lucy Gordon's dramatic *Vengeance Is Mine*, featuring Luke Harmon as Mr. May.

Don't let these men get away!

Yours,

Isabel Swift
Senior Editor & Editorial Coordinator

JOAN JOHNSTON
Marriage by the Book

Silhouette Desire

Published by Silhouette Books New York

America's Publisher of Contemporary Romance

SILHOUETTE BOOKS
300 East 42nd St., New York, N.Y. 10017

ISBN: 0-373-05489-0

First Silhouette Books printing April 1989

Printed in the U.S.A.

Books by Joan Johnston

Silhouette Desire

Fit to Be Tied #424
Marriage by the Book #489

JOAN JOHNSTON

became a closet reader of romances several years ago
and started a habit of hiding one in her briefcase.
Since then she has published several historical novels.
In addition to being an author, she is a lawyer, a
teacher and the mother of two children. In her spare
time she enjoys sailing, horseback riding, and
camping.

For my daughter, Heather Lynne Johnston,
who is bright and beautiful
and has a great sense of fashion.

With love,
Mom

One

———

Her Book: *YOU DON'T HAVE TO STAY SINGLE*
His Book: *HOW TO MARRY THE WOMAN OF
YOUR DREAMS*

Where do you want to do it?" he asked.

"In the shower," she answered with a shy smile.
"It's always been a fantasy of mine, if you want to
know the truth."

She led him to the maroon-and-gray-tiled bathroom. A blush rose on her cheeks as she quickly
stripped the sheer panties and lace bras from the towel
rack where she'd left them to dry. "Sorry about that."

He grinned in that sexy way that had charmed her
from the first moment she'd seen him. His green eyes
were lambent with passion. "You're so beautiful," he

murmured. "I want to see all of you." He tried pulling her T-shirt over her head, but it got caught.

"Wait! Wait! It's stuck on my nose!" She pried the T-shirt off and found his gaze, hot and hard on her. She felt her blood heating up like a prairie fire out of control and thought it was probably a good thing they were getting into the shower. She swallowed over the lump in her throat and said, "Your turn."

He reached down to pull his cotton shirt up and off. At the same time, she reached over to help. His balled fist caught her under the chin, jamming her lower teeth into her lip.

"Ow!"

"Sorry, sweetheart." He couldn't reach out to her because his arms were trapped inside his shirt. "Are you all right?"

She tasted blood, but didn't want to spoil the mood. "It's nothing. Maybe we should undress ourselves."

"Anything you say, darling."

He was out of his tight-fitting jeans and standing naked and ready at the back of the tub by the time she slid out of her short shorts and joined him. Since she was closer, she turned on the shower—which sent out a jet of ice cold water. She yelped and stepped back, slamming an elbow into his stomach.

"Ooomph!"

"Oh, I'm sorry." She stuck her head, sodden hair and all, back under the spray and reached to adjust the temperature, which by now was almost scalding. Finally she got it right and turned to face him, a game smile on her face.

He pressed her up against the tile wall, his strong, muscular body conforming to her soft curves.

She gasped and instantly arched her back so her breasts were forced against the crisp black hair on his chest.

"Whoa, baby," he murmured. "Take it easy. We've got all night . . . or at least until we run out of hot water."

"The wall's freezing!"

"Oh." He stepped back. "How about if I pick you up?" He cupped his hands around her thighs and heaved, but couldn't lift her.

"Must have been that last taco I ate," she teased.

He bent his knees and tried again. This time he got one leg up, but not the other.

"Ow!" she cried.

He quickly released her. "What's the matter now?" he asked, a glint of humor in his eyes.

Chagrined, she admitted, "I got a cramp in my leg."

"Let me help you rub it out."

The sensation of his large hands caressing her leg made her knees feel rubbery. "Uh, keep that up and I'm liable to become a puddle at your feet."

"While we make sure your cramp has gone away for good, how about if I soap you up a bit," he suggested.

"That sounds like fun."

And it was. At last, something that felt as good as she'd imagined. His thumbs grazed her nipples, bringing them erect. His hands curved down over her flat belly and into the nest of curls below. After a heart-stopping foray, they slid back up and around to her buttocks.

"How about giving it another try?" he rasped in her ear. "Ready for me to lift you up?"

She nodded, too breathless to speak.

This time when he reached for her hips he couldn't get a grip at all. Her body was too slippery from soap.

They both laughed. He turned and backed up a little so she could rinse herself off—and hit his head on the shower spigot.

"Ouch!" He let go of her to rub his head.

"Let me help." She reached up toward his temple, but her soapy hand brushed against the edge of his eye.

He quickly squinted and gave a cry of alarm. "Have you got a dry cloth? I've got soap in my eye."

"Just a second and I'll get a towel." She stepped out of the shower with the distinct feeling she'd just escaped from a war zone...until she slipped on the tile floor and nearly went flying. She grappled for the towel rack and barely managed to remain standing.

"Hey! Wake up out there! Where's my towel?"

Megan Padget felt a hand grab her shoulder and shake it. "Wake up! Wake up!"

"I'm awake," she replied, blinking as a piercing light hit her eyes.

"Happy thirty-ninth birthday, Mom!"

Megan sat up abruptly and looked around her. She wasn't anywhere near the shower. She was sitting in the cushioned cane chair in her living room. It had all been a weird, crazy dream. She yawned and rubbed the crick in her neck.

"We finished the dishes, Mom," her fourteen-year-old daughter, Sarah, said.

"And we have a surprise for your birthday," her eight-year-old son, Christopher added.

"You're not going to believe the present we got for you, Mom," Sarah said. "You'll really be surprised!"

"I'm sure you're right." Megan was having a little trouble leaving her dream behind. No one could have that much misfortune in a single attempt to make love with a man in the shower. No wonder she'd never attempted it in real life. Still, it *was* a fantasy of hers.... She'd just have to make sure it never came true in quite that way. Her grin widened as she thought of all the ridiculous things that had gone wrong. She felt the crinkles appear beside her large hazel eyes and around her wide, full mouth. Character lines. A sign of a life well and happily lived, she thought. Even if she never had made love in the shower.

"Hurry up, Mom," Chris urged, pulling her out of the chair. "We made a cake for you. C'mon and light the candles."

As she followed her children into the dining room, Megan ran a hand through her shoulder-length, golden brown hair. In the past year she'd noticed some gray here and there. Yes, she was definitely going to be thirty-nine this year. She took the book of matches Sarah handed to her. "This is a beautiful chocolate cake, Sarah. Did you make it all by yourself?"

"I helped with the icing," Chris said.

Sarah grimaced at her brother. "Right. He licked the eggbeaters clean."

"Aw, Mom!"

Megan reached over and ruffled Chris's towhead of hair, a legacy from his father. Sarah's hair was equally straight and blond, thanks to the hours she spent in the warm Miami sun. Megan's children were beautiful, bright and precocious, and she felt a swell of pride and love that they'd remembered her birthday in such a special way.

"Thanks to both of you for cleaning up the kitchen while I napped. And you've made me a beautiful chocolate cake! This has been the best birthday ever."

"You haven't even opened your present yet," Sarah protested.

"I'm sure I'll love whatever you two got for me."

Unable to sit calmly any longer, Chris got up from his chair and came to stand beside her. His face flushed as he handed her an elaborately wrapped gift. "Open it, Mom."

"It feels heavy," Megan said. "I wonder what it could be."

"It's a book!" Chris blurted out.

"Shut up, Chris! Mom, he always spoils everything!"

"I do not!"

"You do so!"

"That's enough, Sarah."

"Do not!" Chris retorted one last time.

Megan waited until Chris was seated at the table again before she said, "Nothing is spoiled, Sarah, because I don't know which book you two have bought for me. Do you want me to guess before I open it?"

"You'll never guess in a million years," Sarah said, the beatific smile returning to her face.

"Yeah, never in a million years," Chris agreed.

"Chris," Sarah warned.

"I never said anything!"

Megan ignored the sibling argument and concentrated on the weight of the hardbound book in her hands. She couldn't help but wonder what her children had chosen for her. She'd been reading a lot of bestsellers lately, and she suspected they'd purchased the latest spy thriller.

"It's a suspense novel," Megan guessed.

"Wrong!" Sarah said with a pleased giggle. "Hurry up and open it, Mom. I can't wait to see what you think."

Megan tore the paper off, genuinely curious to see what Sarah and Chris had bought. "Oh, my God! Sarah, this is . . . this is . . ."

"It's a book about how to find a husband, Mom. See?"

Megan saw only too well. *YOU DON'T HAVE TO STAY SINGLE* was staring at her in bold print and capital letters. Megan didn't know what to say. She was flabbergasted. She'd had no idea her children still had hopes of her marrying and providing them with a father. She'd divorced Gary five years ago, and in the years since then the right man had never come along.

After literally thousands of dates—well, perhaps only sixty-three or so, but who was counting?—she'd thought her children had become as discouraged as she was. Apparently not.

She realized she still hadn't thanked her children. Luckily, Sarah was so excited she was still talking nonstop.

"…So you see, Mom, you've been going about this husband-hunting business all wrong. This book has step-by-step instructions, and there's even a money-back guarantee if you aren't married within a year of the date you purchased the book."

Megan felt an envelope being pressed into her hand.

"The receipt for the book is in this envelope," Sarah explained. "But I'll bet anything you never have to send it in."

"You gotta read this book, Mom," Christopher piped up. "'Cause I just gotta have someone besides my mom to play football with me. I mean, how's it gonna look when I'm in junior high school someday and still tackling you?"

"All right," Megan said with a rueful smile. "I promise to read it." She flipped open the book and began perusing the chapter headings. She flushed when she read the title of Chapter Five, "Sex—Don't Jump the Gun."

"Sarah, how much of this did you read before you wrapped it up?"

Sarah grinned. "I checked it all out, Mom. *Especially* Chapter Five."

"You're too young—"

"Jeez, Mom. We've had sex education in school. There wasn't anything there that I didn't already know. But there were a few suggestions—"

"That'll be all for now, young lady," Megan said, taking note of her wide-eyed, big-eared son.

"Sure, Mom," Sarah said. "And when you read Chapter Two I'd really like to talk with you. I think I could be a big help."

Megan looked down at the heading for Chapter Two, "Dressing for *Sex*cess," and flushed again. But she had to agree her daughter was probably right. Sarah spent hours poring over the fashions in her teen magazines and eagerly put the ideas she read about into practice. Megan had often marveled at how Sarah could take a blouse, a belt, a scarf, floppy-topped socks and a pair of jeans and turn the ensemble into a fashion statement.

It was hard to accept the fact that her daughter wasn't a child anymore. In just four years she'd be going off to college. It wouldn't be long before Chris would follow in her footsteps. Was it possible Sarah had worried that her mother would be alone in the years to come and had sought a way to remedy that situation? Sometimes Sarah acted so . . . adult.

Megan set the book down on the table before she stood and pulled Chris into her arms for a quick hug. He resisted the closeness, as Megan had known he would. Sarah was only slightly more cooperative when her turn came.

"Thanks, honey," Megan said. "I mean it. I'm going to start reading tonight, and when I get to Chapter Two I'll let you know."

"You still haven't lit the candles," Chris said, holding up the box of matches.

Thirty-nine candles created quite a blaze, and by the time Megan got the last one lit the first had started to leave a large wax puddle on the icing.

"Quick! Make a wish and blow them out!" Sarah said.

Megan closed her eyes and wished for "the right man" to come along. Then she took a deep, hopeful breath and blew hard.

"You got 'em all, Mom!" Chris shouted. "Every last one!"

"What did you wish for?" Sarah asked.

"You know you can't tell a wish or it won't come true," Chris countered. "What *did* you wish for, Mom?"

Megan smiled broadly. "You know I can't tell you that."

Her children settled for a piece of cake topped with ice cream, and by the time they got the dishes done and the wrapping paper and ribbon picked up it was late.

"I think you two had better think about getting to bed," Megan said. "You've both got school tomorrow."

"Aw, Mom."

"Bed, Christopher," Megan said firmly.

"Good night, Mom," Sarah said. "I've got some more studying to do before I turn out the light, but will you come and tuck me in?"

Megan smiled. There was still a little bit of the child left in Sarah and she'd gladly nourish it for as long as it lasted. "Sure, honey. Just give me a call when you get your contact lenses out and your glasses on."

Christopher had already disappeared into his room when Megan called after him, "Don't forget to brush your teeth, Chris."

"Aw, Mom."

"Teeth, Christopher."

In a very short time Sarah was tucked in and the house was dark and quiet. Doing the last minute straightening around the house, Megan came across *YOU DON'T HAVE TO STAY SINGLE* on the dining-room table. As an educator, she was the first to acknowledge the power of books to alter viewpoints, increase knowledge and shape attitudes and opinions. But reading a book to find out how to land a husband seemed to be carrying things a bit too far.

"But I promised I'd look at it," she said with a disbelieving shake of her head, "and I will."

She carried *YOU DON'T HAVE TO STAY SINGLE* with her to her femininely-decorated bedroom and set it on the table beside the bed. She debated whether or not to wear the sexy nightgown her best friend, Stephanie Stobs, had given her for her birthday, but finally gave in to the need to feel the cool, silky fabric against her skin. She pulled down the sheets and climbed into the same queen-size bed she'd slept in for the last five years of her marriage and the five years since. It sagged a little in the middle, but there was no one to run into when she landed in the center at night, so she couldn't see replacing it.

She fluffed up her two pillows and leaned back against the headboard with the book in her lap. She perused the chapter headings again: "Meeting Your Man"; "Dressing for *Sex*cess"; "You *Can* Ask Him Out!"; "Sex—Don't Jump the Gun"; "Meeting His Mother" and "Getting Him to Pop the Question." It all looked pretty harmless. But was it going to be helpful?

Megan paged through the introduction and dedication until she got to Chapter One. She read:

> *You go exploring for oil in a place where you expect to find it. The same holds true when looking for "the right man."*
>
> *The most common place for a woman to meet the man she will marry is the workplace. It stands to reason that a woman who works in a career that attracts men will have the best chance of meeting "the right man."*

Megan laughed aloud as she perused the list of suggested occupations: plumber, telephone lineman, elevator inspector, men's shoe salesman, IRS agent, automobile salesman, boat-repair-and-service technician and politician.

"What's so funny, Mom?" Sarah called from her bedroom.

"Nothing, honey. I just thought of a joke I heard today." She didn't have the heart to tell Sarah how ridiculous the book was. She swallowed her own disappointment as she put it on the bedside table and turned off the lamp.

Yanking the covers up over her bare shoulders she thought about her job at St. Mark's University. She was a good teacher and her responsibilities as chairman of the science department challenged her. The atmosphere at the university was friendly and supportive. But the St. Mark's faculty left a lot to be desired as a source of eligible males. She was a lot more likely to find a *father* on campus than a *husband!*

Thomas Steele eyed the thirty-five flaming candles on his birthday cake with something less than enthusiasm.

"All right, Tom. Make a wish and blow them out," his older brother, Randy, urged.

"Wish for something good," Randy's wife, Irene, added.

Tom stood for long seconds thinking what he wanted most out of life—and came up with a blank. He liked making love at dawn, sailing in a storm, popcorn and beer, sleeping late in the rain with the feel of a soft woman curved against his hard body, and slow, deep kisses. The problem was he felt a vague sense of dissatisfaction with his life and couldn't seem to locate the source. When the candles began to puddle on the cake he gave up and blew them out without deciding on anything.

"What did you wish for?" Randy asked.

"A hundred-foot yacht and the time and money to sail it to Tahiti," Tom quipped with a grin.

It had been a longstanding dream for the two brothers to sail away into the sunset. Their lives had been grim enough to demand a dream to sustain them. Their alcoholic father had regularly beaten their mother, and when he was finished with her he'd started on them. When the policeman had come to the door to report their father's death in a drunk driving accident, their mother had wept, and so had Tom and Randy. The policeman had been sympathetic to what he supposed was their grief. But fourteen-year-old Tom and seventeen-year-old Randy had been shedding guilty tears of relief.

Tom had sworn then that he'd never hurt a woman the way his father had hurt his mother. And he hadn't. His initial solution to the problem had been to avoid women altogether. During his adolescent years, the time when most young men honed their skills in male-female relationships, Tom hadn't dated. As he'd matured, however, his dark good looks had drawn women to him like metal filings to a magnet. Tom had accepted their freely offered feminine gifts, but he'd been careful never to lose control of his emotions with a woman. The fear was always there that if he did, he might discover he was capable of the same destructive violence as his father.

When the time had come to marry, he hadn't been a good husband. He'd learned too late that he kept too much of himself hidden away from his wife. Sally had begged him to let go, to share his thoughts and feelings, but he hadn't been able to do it. When Sally had divorced him he'd been forced to admit that his fierce control on his emotions had made him seem cold to her when she needed him most—because the times when he was feeling the most were the times when the fear he might do violence to his wife rose up to haunt him. It didn't seem to matter that he'd never raised a hand to her. The fear was there.

Unfortunately, his efforts in adolescence to avoid his fear by avoiding women, had created another problem that was equally frustrating to Tom. For what appeared on the surface to be simple reserve with women, was in fact, painful shyness. To his utter chagrin, his tongue was tied by adolescent awkwardness when he attempted a conversation with a woman to whom he was deeply attracted.

"Hey, what's got you so serious?" Randy asked, chewing a mouthful of the cake Irene had served to him. "I'd give my eyeteeth to have looked half as good as you do now when I was thirty-five."

Tom flushed. "Cut it out, Randy."

Randy leaned back in the large, comfortable chair in Tom's living room and took a sip of his beer. "Face it. You're a hunk."

"He's right," Irene seconded from her seat on the couch. "You've got those sexy green eyes and that wavy black hair. You're tall, with broad shoulders and lean hips."

"Cut it out, Irene. You're embarrassing me," Tom said.

"Don't try to pretend you don't know you're good-looking. We're not going to buy it," Randy said. "If I were you—and I weren't already married to a wonderful woman—I'd be taking a little more advantage of all that female attention."

Tom's lips twisted in a sardonic smile. "You'd be amazed what a difference it makes to a woman when she realizes I'm not interested in a long-term relationship."

"How well I remember." Randy reached out to grasp Irene's hand. "That's why Irene and I got you a very special birthday present this year—something that's going to change your life."

"Oh, yeah? If it isn't season tickets for the Miami Dolphins, forget it." Tom put his feet up against the edge of the ancient Formica dining-room table that had come with the furnished apartment he'd rented when he'd arrived in Miami two weeks ago. He leaned back until his chair rested on only two of its aluminum legs.

Randy retrieved a hastily wrapped gift from the table in front of him and threw it across the room to his brother. "Here. Open it."

Tom took his time opening the present. When he had enough wrapping paper removed to see what was in his hands his facial muscles tightened. His feet came off the table and the chair clunked down on all four legs. "What the hell is this?"

"Now don't get upset," Irene said soothingly. "Randy and I were only thinking—"

"It's pretty clear from this gift what you were thinking. But you were wrong." Tom threw the half-unwrapped book on the table. "I'm not interested in finding a wife now or in the future."

"I know you think you failed Sally," Randy said. "And you got burned pretty badly by your breakup with Maryanne."

"To a crisp."

"That's no reason to give up on everything marriage has to offer. I made a mistake the first go-around, too." Randy's hand tightened around Irene's. "But I found that things were different with the right partner. It's high time you found yourself a good woman and settled down."

"I haven't had the time—or the inclination—since Maryanne turned down my proposal."

"You can't keep running from marriage, Tom."

"I'm not running from anything. Has it occurred to you that I've just never found the right woman?"

Randy's jaw dropped open and a grin split his face. "Well, well, well. Then Irene and I have chosen a good present after all. This book is *guaranteed* to help you marry the woman of your dreams." He handed Tom an envelope. "The receipt's in here. Just hang on to it for a year, and if you aren't married you get a full refund. How about that for a deal?"

Tom laughed. "I give up. Give me the damn thing."

Randy picked up the book and held it out to Tom.

Tom shook his head in disbelief as he accepted the birthday gift from his brother. *"HOW TO MARRY THE WOMAN OF YOUR DREAMS.* Pretty heady stuff. You don't honestly believe that a book like this is going to make a difference, do you?''

Randy grinned and winked at Irene. "Sure I do. It worked for me.''

Tom gaped at Randy. "You used this to find Irene?''

"He had Chapter Three down pat," Irene said. "I fell for him hook, line and sinker.''

Tom perused the chapter headings until he found the one Irene had referred to: "Sex—When to Make Your Move." When he looked back up Irene was blushing.

Randy pulled his wife to her feet. He wrapped his arms around her and gave her a crushing squeeze. "God, I love you, woman!" Randy kept his arms around Irene as he turned and spoke to Tom. "I can't make you read that book. But as your older brother I'm giving you some good advice. Don't knock it till you've tried it. Now I think it's time we headed for home.''

He kept an arm around Irene's waist as he walked over to lay a hand affectionately on Tom's shoulder. "Happy birthday. It's great having you here in Miami, even if it's only for the next nine months. I'll call you later this week and we'll get together for lunch. I want to hear how you like your new job.''

"Sounds good to me." Tom rose and gave his sister-in-law a kiss on the cheek. "Thank you both. I appreciate you baking a cake for me, Irene.''

"I enjoyed it, but maybe this time next year you'll have your own special someone to bake one for you.''

Tom's lips flattened. "Yeah. Sure."

"Read it!" Randy called over his shoulder as he and Irene stepped out the door.

When they were gone, Tom looked down at the book in his hand. Well, it couldn't hurt to glance at it. Then he could face Randy with a clear conscience.

He carried the book over to the one chair in the living room, a huge, overstuffed corduroy monstrosity, and sat down, putting his bare feet up on an equally huge ottoman in front of it. He quickly reviewed the chapters: "Where to Meet Your Dream Woman"; "That First Fabulous Date"; "Sex—When to Make Your Move"; "What Do Her Criticisms Mean?"; "Avoiding Cold Feet When It's Time to Commit" and "Putting the Ring on Her Finger."

He had to admit there appeared to be a lot of useful information in the book. He resisted the urge to check out the chapter on sex, and began reading at the beginning.

Women are everywhere.

Tom laughed aloud. He didn't need a book to tell him that.

The problem is how to make contact with them. You'll do best opening a conversation with a woman if you have a reason for speaking to her. Thus service industries make excellent occupa-

tions for single men anxious to meet a prospective wife.

Tom read through the list of industries that put a man in contact with women and had to laugh again. Vacuum-cleaner salesman, hairdresser, manicurist, women's shoe salesman, principal, aerobics instructor—he couldn't fault the list, but where did that leave him? He taught college classes in political science and advised a lot of high-powered politicans. Unfortunately his female students were all much too young for him, and the vast majority of the politicans he advised were male.

He didn't want to change his job. He liked his work, and he was looking forward to his new position as a visiting professor in the political science department at St. Mark's University. He closed the book and tossed it onto the coffee table. He leaned back in the corduroy chair and crossed his forearms over his brow.

He wasn't averse to the idea of marriage, but the truth was he had too much trouble talking with women to hope that he'd be successful finding a wife on the basis of what he learned in a book. In fact, the idea of using a book to find the woman of his dreams struck him as ridiculous. Except that, as a teacher, he knew that only a fool discounted the power of the printed word. Besides, it had supposedly worked for Randy.

He remembered the feeling of dissatisfaction that had plagued him lately. Was it a *woman* that was missing from his life? Maybe it was. He toyed with the idea of taking this book seriously, then shook his head in chagrin. He couldn't believe how far he'd let his whimsy carry him. Maybe he'd find the woman of his dreams at St. Mark's, but it was more likely she'd remain a figment of his imagination.

He forced himself to get up and go into the bedroom to sleep. Not that there was anyone to know or care where he spent the night, but he'd found it was easier to rest if he maintained a semblance of normalcy. He fell asleep almost immediately. And he dreamed. There was a woman with warm, brown eyes, laughing delightedly, her face tilted up for his kiss . . . and they were in the shower.

Two

___

Her Book: "Meeting Your Man"
His Book: "Where to Meet Your Dream Woman"

Your children got you *what* for your birthday?"

"Keep your voice down, Stephanie. Somebody's likely to hear you." Megan looked around the room filled with professors who'd gathered for the annual welcome address by the president of St. Mark's University. There were more than a hundred members of the faculty and staff stuffed in the small auditorium like candy in a kid's mouth.

Stephanie Stobs was an associate professor in the art department and Megan's closest friend. One of the things Megan liked most about her was her vivacious personality, but Stephanie had a distinctive voice and it carried easily. Megan leaned over and whispered in her friend's ear, "You heard me. I said they bought me a book called, *YOU DON'T HAVE TO STAY SINGLE*."

"Lordy, Lordy! I didn't know you were still looking for a husband."

"Shh! I'm not. At least, I wasn't until I got this book. Now I have to at least make a token effort at dating or I'm going to hurt their feelings. The book is full of how-to advice you wouldn't believe."

"I hope you're planning to share all the good stuff with me," Stephanie said with a grin.

"I'm not sure how much good stuff there is. Unless you'd like to consider becoming a men's shoe salesman."

Stephanie frowned, perplexed. "A men's shoe salesman?"

At that moment Steven Sawyer, the dean for academic affairs, called the meeting to order. For the next two hours they sat through mundane announcements about what had happened over the past summer and what the administration planned for the coming year. The president, Father John O'Hara, gave an inspirational speech designed to get everyone off on the right foot, and the morning session ended with the introduction of each new member of the faculty.

Megan was half paying attention, doodling daisies on her notepad, when Stephanie jabbed her in the ribs. "Will you look at that!"

Megan stared at the man standing toward the front of the auditorium. He was tall and lean, and had dark hair that just trailed over the collar of his pale pink, short-sleeved shirt. He wore form-fitting gray trousers that, from the back, left little to the imagination. Not the typical St. Mark's professor. Not at all!

At that moment he turned to gesture toward the man sitting beside him and Megan got a good look at his face.

"Lordy, Lordy!" Stephanie chanted. "Where did he come from?"

Megan couldn't answer because all the air had just been sucked from her lungs. He couldn't be as good-looking as she thought he was. She blinked her eyes, but he remained just as striking. His strong profile showed a once-straight nose that looked as though it had been broken several times, the slightly jutting chin of a man used to getting his way, high, sharp cheekbones and half of a wide, friendly smile that was devastating even from where she sat.

"Who is he?" Megan asked. "Did you hear his name?"

"Tom, I think," Stephanie murmured. "I can't believe a gorgeous guy like that is joining our faculty. I'll bet he's married. No guy that good-looking is still single. Unless he...no, he's just got to be straight. He's too good to be true! I can't wait to meet him."

"And Tom will be a visiting professor this year," Dean Sawyer intoned. "He comes to us from Washington, D.C., where he's the chairman of the political science department at Georgetown University. Tom is frequently called upon as a consultant to the U.S. State Department for his expertise on South American affairs. We're proud and pleased to welcome Tom to the faculty of St. Mark's for the coming year."

"I should have known," Stephanie grumbled. "He's only visiting." Then she grinned. "But he's here for a whole year. That means I've got a shot at convincing him that Miami has a lot to offer a man—starting with me!"

Megan realized that Stephanie was exactly the sort of woman a hunk like Tom Whatever would go for. She was dark eyed, dark haired and dazzling. Megan, at thirty-nine, didn't even put herself in the same class with Stephanie, who was ten years younger. And if Stephanie had set her sights on Tom Something-or-Other, the chances were good that she would land him. From Stephanie's next words, it was clear she was already plotting her seduction.

"Look, the whole faculty's supposed to have lunch in the cafeteria," she said. "Let's make sure we sit at the same table as Tom."

"I already promised to sit with Dean Sawyer," Megan replied, unable to completely keep the disappointment from her voice. "I need to talk with him about some budget matters. I guess you're on your own—you and the rest of the single female faculty."

Stephanie's eyes sparkled with mischief. "Think I'm gonna have some competition?"

"Don't you?"

"Yeah. But I'm up to the challenge."

Megan couldn't disagree. Stephanie was dressed in a bright blue silk dress that emphasized her small waist and generous bosom. She wore sexy high heels to compensate for her lack of height. Add dynamite looks to Stephanie's outgoing personality and what man could resist her? Certainly not Tom What's-His-Name, she thought glumly.

"I'll see you later," Stephanie said as the crowd began to disperse for lunch. "I've got to get going so I can be somewhere near him in the serving line."

Megan sighed. She looked down at her own attire and felt a sense of futility. The cotton knit dress had been washed so often that the vibrant primary colors in the print were faded. The dress fit, but with the bloused bodice it completely hid a more than respectable figure. The midcalf length of the skirt left no more than five or six inches of her legs visible. She'd long ago eschewed sexy high heels for comfortable pumps. She looked downright . . . dowdy.

She grimaced at the thought of how she must be flunking the chapter on "Dressing for *Sex*cess" in her birthday book. Her daughter had been right to think that she might need some help. The question was whether it was too late to put all that excellent advice to good use.

Megan joined Dean Sawyer's table with her lunch tray and argued with him for most of the lunch hour over the money she needed for some lab equipment. Her diplomatic skills had helped her become chairman of the science department, and she'd used them to good effect over the past few years to keep the department's resources up-to-date. But this time Dean Sawyer wasn't cooperating.

"If we don't get those new filters, the microsensors we have are going to wear out much sooner. It makes good sense to order the filters now instead of waiting," Megan said.

"I understand your position," Dean Sawyer replied, "but I have other priorities right now."

Megan felt herself losing her temper, but couldn't seem to get control. "You're making a big mistake, and you're not going to appreciate it in a year when—"

"I've made my decision, Megan. It's final."

"Damn, damn, damn!" Megan muttered under her breath. She could feel the tears behind her eyelids. Why was she getting so upset over some lousy equipment? At that moment she looked away and straight into Tom What's-His-Name's eyes.

He was staring at her with green-gray orbs the color of a deep, sunlit sea. He seemed to be searching her face for answers. *And I don't even know the questions.* She examined his face for some sign of his reaction to her and was surprised to find desire—and distrust.

She couldn't look away from him. His lashes were long and too lush for a man's. His brows were straight with only a slight curve at the ends that forced her attention back to those enigmatic eyes. Despite the fact that the day was only half-done, a light shadow of beard defined his jaw. She wanted to look away, but couldn't.

She felt her heartbeat kick into high gear as his gaze moved to her lips. She let her glance drift to his mouth and saw that it was wide, with slightly full, parted lips.

She imagined those lips on hers, felt the soft pressure of that wide mouth closing over her own, imagined his tongue sliding along her lips to tease and taunt her. Her whole body shivered with pleasure at the thought. She watched as his mouth curved into a knowing smile.

Her gaze slid back to his lambent eyes, now the deep, dark green of a stormy sea. Mortified, she realized that he'd guessed her thoughts. She blushed bright red as she looked down at the food left on her tray. Had she actually been imagining a perfect stranger's lips on her own? What in the world was the matter with her?

In the first place, Stephanie had already staked her claims on the man. She would be a fool to try and compete with the younger woman. And speaking of younger, Tom Whoever-He-Was certainly didn't look thirty-nine. How could she be having such carnal thoughts about a younger man? She sneaked a peek at him from under her lashes and saw that he'd turned his attention to his companion on the left—who just happened to be Stephanie. Stephanie spoke animatedly to him and he was nodding and smiling in return.

Forget it, Megan. You're asking for trouble if you even look at the man again.

But dear God in heaven, when was the last time she'd felt anything so sexually enticing, so wickedly wonderful, when she'd simply looked at a man? She was actually considering competing with Stephanie for his attention. And why not? He was certainly worth it. The first thing she was going to do when she got home was check out Chapter Two of her birthday book. Just see if she didn't provide a little competition for Stephanie when she was dressed for *sex*cess!

When Stephanie joined Megan again for the afternoon session in the auditorium, she was full of compliments for Tom, whose last name she'd learned was Steele.

"He's got the sexiest voice. It's low and quiet, but he doesn't use it often. What I mean to say is, he doesn't talk much. All I could find out is that he plans to take advantage of his South American contacts here in Miami for some paper he's working on this coming year. He wasn't wearing a ring, but I asked him if he was married, anyway."

Stephanie paused and turned to Megan, who waited with bated breath until her friend said, "He's divorced. But he didn't volunteer any other information about himself. He's kind of quiet for being such a hunk. But that only makes him more attractive, don't you think?"

"He is attractive," Megan admitted. "In fact, I think he's the most attractive man I've seen in a long time."

Stephanie's brows rose. "Oh? Well, I think the feeling is mutual."

"What?"

"I said I think he finds you attractive, too."

"How can you say such a thing," Megan chided. "He was sitting with you."

"But he was looking at *you*," Stephanie pointed out. "In fact, he couldn't take his eyes off you. He even asked me your name."

Megan felt the color rising in her cheeks. "He did?"

"Uh huh."

"Oh."

"I saw you staring at him, Megan. It was love at first sight. You're crazy about him already, aren't you?"

"So what if I am?" she answered defensively. "What's wrong with that?"

"Why, nothing. I say go for it."

Megan wrung her hands in her lap. "But I thought you planned...uh...wanted—"

"Look, Megan, you know how it is. Either the chemistry's there or it isn't. I think Tom's a great-looking guy. I'd give it a go, but it's plain as the cute little nose on your face that he's not the least bit interested in me. Anyway, while I was eating I got a good look at the new football coach. Ooo la la! So I wish you the best with Tom. In fact, if there's anything I can do to help things along, just let me know."

"Um, well, there is something, actually."

"Name it."

"I may need your help doing some clothes shopping this weekend. You see there's this chapter in my birthday book on how to dress especially to attract a man. I'd appreciate your input when I'm ready to hit the stores."

"Sure. I'm free on Saturday. We have that faculty reception at the president's house on Sunday. You'll want to wear something stunning when you talk with Tom for the first time."

"Maybe he won't be there," Megan said.

"He'll show. It's required for new faculty. It's a come-and-go affair, though, so we'll have to be sure to get there early so you don't miss him."

Megan shook her head in disbelief. "I don't believe I'm doing this."

"It's about time. You've been out of action long enough. Megan Padget rides again!"

"Good grief, Stephanie. You make me sound like the Lone Ranger."

"Well, it's going to take more than a silver bullet to get this man. Something tells me Thomas Steele is more elusive than your ordinary bachelor."

At that moment Dean Sawyer called the afternoon session to order. Megan was grateful for the interruption because she didn't want to think about how hard it was going to be to garner Thomas Steele's attention. After all, it wasn't as though she really had hopes of developing a serious relationship with him. He was only going to be in Miami for a year. And it had been so long since she'd gone out on a date she'd probably forgotten all the rules. But at least if she saw him once or twice and nothing came of it her children would be convinced that she'd given it her best shot and allow her to send in her birthday book receipt for a refund. Then she could buy the latest mystery bestseller and retire to her comfortable bed for an exciting night of reading.

Tom had found out the woman's name was Megan Padget. He hadn't wanted to ask too many questions, because he didn't want to make his interest in her more obvious than he feared it already was. Truthfully, he found her more than a little intriguing. He'd felt her eyes on him a couple of times before he'd finally found her in the crowd at the dean's table. There was something about her that called to his senses. Her eyes were large and brown, like milk chocolate. Her hair was kind of a dark honey blond with curls that bounced when she talked. Strawberry-pink lips pouted slightly, and her complexion was pure whipped cream. Chocolate. Honey. Strawberries. Whipped cream. His mouth watered just thinking about her. He'd always had a sweet tooth, and God, she was bound to taste delicious!

Before he could start daydreaming about her again he picked up the phone in his living room and dialed Randy's number. Irene answered and he gave her an abbreviated version of the day before Randy came on the line.

"So, did you meet the woman of your dreams today?"

"Yes."

There was a stunned silence on the phone as Randy absorbed what his brother had said before the receiver erupted in Tom's ear. "I'll be damned, little brother! When you make up your mind to do something you don't fool around, do you?"

Tom stood there grinning like an idiot, glad Randy couldn't see the silly expression on his face. "It's hardly as though I went searching for the woman, Randy. She was just there."

"I assume she teaches at St. Mark's?"

"She's the chairman of the science department."

"Science, huh? Do you suppose she likes experimenting with new things?" Randy asked, his voice full of innuendo.

Tom felt warmth rising on his face as he remembered that he'd already imagined Megan Padget wrapped around him a dozen different ways. He cleared his throat and said, "Don't get your hopes up, Randy. She's probably married with a couple of kids."

"You mean you didn't ask her?"

"I haven't even spoken to her yet."

There was a dead silence on the phone. Finally Randy said, "You must have it bad, little brother, if you can call her the woman of your dreams when you haven't even exchanged the time of day. She must be a real stunner."

"She's got luscious features, but it was hard to tell about her figure or her height. The only time I saw her she was sitting down. I waited as long as I could for her to stand up, but I had to leave with the crowd at lunch or it would have been obvious that I was looking at her. When I tried to find her later she was gone."

"When are you going to see her again?"

"There's a faculty reception at the president's house on Sunday. I suppose I'll see her there."

"Are you going to ask her out on a date?"

This time it was Tom's end of the line that remained silent. Was he going to pursue Megan Padget? He thought of how sweet she'd looked. Then he thought of how quickly things had gone sour with Sally and Maryanne. Was the promise of a good marriage worth the risk of pain if he let himself get involved with the woman? He sighed and answered, "I don't know."

"Look, I hate to sound like a broken record," Randy said, "but there's more to life than politics and sailing. You're by yourself too much, Tom, and that isn't healthy."

"I'm sure I'll make friends I can spend time with."

Randy snorted. "And a lot of those 'friends' will be female. Don't think I don't know it. But I'm talking about the kind of woman you seek out when you think about having a family, making a home for yourself. You must have wanted it once upon a time or you wouldn't have been so torn up when you lost Sally and Maryanne got away."

"Randy, I—"

"All I'm asking is that you think about it," Randy said. "Don't judge every woman by your experience with those two. All women are not the same. Take it from me."

Tom brushed a hand through his thick black hair, thrusting it from his forehead. "All right, Randy. I'll think about it."

"That's all I'm asking. Just imagine spending the rest of your life with the woman of your dreams."

Tom hung up the phone and sagged into his chair. What could it hurt to ask her out on a date? Still, he knew he was going to have trouble talking to her. He was too attracted to her for it to be otherwise. Maybe he'd just put the moves on her, take her to bed and get her out of his system, as he had done with the others in the years since Maryanne. Hell, anything more than that was asking for trouble.

But the vague sense of dissatisfaction prickling at his neck bothered him. He brushed a hand through his rumpled hair as though to wipe the feeling away. Then he picked up *HOW TO MARRY THE WOMAN OF YOUR DREAMS* from the spooled coffee table and paged through it until he got to the chapter entitled, "That First Fabulous Date." He settled back in the comfortable corduroy chair and started to read.

Three

———

Megan was frantic. How could she have let her daughter talk her into this? Sarah's arguments had seemed perfectly rational at home. It was only now that she'd taken an assortment of clothing into the dressing room that she began to realize the true folly of this whole scheme. She couldn't shop for sexy clothes with her fourteen-year-old daughter! What kind of message would that send to Sarah's tender young psyche? But when Stephanie had called to say she had some kind of stomach flu, she'd told Megan to go shopping without her. And Sarah, who'd over-heard the conversation, had insisted that she could do as good a job as Stephanie at helping her mom find just the right kind of outfits to be dressed for *sex*cess.

"Are you ready yet, Mom?"

"I'll be out in a minute, Sarah."

Megan looked down at the bright red silk confection she was wearing. Her birthday book had suggested she buy only primary colors. Red sent a pretty basic message, all right. Hot, it said. Ready for sex, it said. I'm woman enough for your man, it said. Megan rolled her eyes. She wasn't sure she was ready to handle the kind of sexual action this dress promised to get for her.

She buttoned up the form-fitting bodice and looked at herself in the mirror. She recalled her birthday book's advice:

Always buy clothing that looks easy to remove. Watch for items that have buttons or laces or zippers down the front. Leave a button or two undone. That way a man can easily imagine himself undressing you. Of course, a T-shirt without a bra has its own allure. Everyone knows how quickly a T-shirt can hit the floor.

She wasn't about to wear a T-shirt to the faculty reception, but then she wasn't so sure about this red dress, either. Tentatively she unbuttoned the first button, and then the second. The dress fell open provocatively. She swung her hips and the full skirt flowed around her. Lord in heaven! She actually looked... sexy.

Her book had also suggested buying touchable fabrics such as silk, wool and cotton. She fingered the silky material, pressed it down across her body, felt its smoothness against her skin. She had to admit it felt sensual. The book had said:

> *You want a man to imagine his fingertips roaming the territory. What is he going to feel? Your clothing should suggest the softness of skin, the textures of sex.*

The textures of sex? Sex wasn't always the texture of silk to Megan's way of thinking. The act of love grew out of the feelings two people had for one another—and as a woman who'd been married for ten years, she knew that often sex between two people reflected feelings that weren't the least bit silky.

Sometimes it was rough, but fun, like terry cloth, a roller coaster of ups and downs like Harris Tweed or rich and full like brocade. There were other times it was adventuresome, like dungaree. There was a definite difference between sex that was soft and delicate like velveteen, and sex that was soft and wild like doeskin. Megan remembered a few snug fits—like banlon, and embraces tight as corseting. Then there were the warm and tender moments like flannel. She'd had her share of stiff buckram sex, too. But her favorite...her favorite sex was cotton. It was natural and honest and durable. And it lasted forever with care.

"Mom? Did you fall asleep in there?"

"I'll be out in a second." But it was several minutes before Megan finally made it out of the dressing room. "Here I am. Well, what do you think?"

"I think you look fantastic."

Megan whirled to find the source of the deep masculine voice. She stared unbelievingly at Tom Steele leaning casually against a wall of the department store. A sleeveless gray T-shirt revealed his muscular arms and the strength of his equally muscular chest. His lean, jeans-clad legs were crossed at his bare ankles, his feet encased in well-worn dock-siders.

"What are you doing here?" she demanded.

"Shopping."

"In ladies clothing?" Megan was upset because she'd dressed to attract him, and didn't know how to handle herself now that he'd shown up in the flesh. It had been over a year since she'd last flirted with a man.

The grin that spread across his face was one of pure male appreciation as he straightened and walked toward her. "I came to pick up my sister-in-law, Irene. She's here somewhere trying on a few things."

Megan hadn't realized how totally focused she'd been on Tom until she realized Sarah had disappeared. She looked around and saw her daughter on the far side of the store talking with one of her girlfriends from school.

"We haven't been formally introduced. I'm Tom Steele."

Megan held her breath in anticipation as Tom extended his hand to her. His large, callused palm surrounded hers and his fingers grasped hers firmly for a moment before he released his grip. The shock was electric and raced up her arm. It was all she could do not to jerk her hand away.

"I'm Megan Padget. It's nice to meet you, Dr. Steele."

"Tom."

"Tom." Megan's lips curved in a smile of genuine pleasure.

Then Tom and Megan just stood and stared at one another. His gaze rested on her face for a moment before it drifted down to her throat. The red dress bared her to his gaze. She groped self-consciously for the buttons she'd unfastened. As she fingered one of the few still buttoned, it slipped loose and the dress fell even further open, revealing the rounded flesh of her breasts. She immediately grabbed a handful of the silk in a wad at her throat. Surely he didn't think she'd done that on purpose!

Tom's eyes took on a hooded look as his glance slid back to her face. His gaze was intense, his eyes dark. She wondered if he was imagining himself undressing her, as the book had said he would. How did he see her?

She felt her nipples pucker beneath the silk, painfully aware that with the new sheer bra she'd bought her arousal must be showing through the dress. Her lips opened to sip a shallow breath of air. She was caught up in a sensual fantasy that could have only one ending.

Megan caught a glimpse of Sarah across the store, sorting through a table of designer blue jeans, and stiffened. How could she have so completely forgotten her daughter's presence! This was no time to let her imagination run amok. As much as she was enjoying it, she needed to get this meeting over with before Sarah returned and started asking embarrassing questions.

"It's..." Her voice was a croak. She cleared her throat and tried again. "It's an honor to have someone with your credentials teaching at St. Mark's this year. You mentioned you're meeting your sister-in-law. Does that mean you have family living here in Miami?"

"My brother, Randy, and his wife."

"She's the one you're meeting?"

"Yes. Is your husband shopping somewhere in the mall?" Tom could have kicked himself for asking such an obvious question. Where was his savoir faire? Not to mention his subtlety. It had been a long time since he'd been so attracted to a woman, and naturally, his brain couldn't seem to get an intelligent message to his mouth.

"Um...my ex-husband died two years ago. I'm not married." Megan groaned inwardly. Dumb, dumb, dumb! Of course she wasn't married if Gary was her *ex*-husband. Did she have to announce her availability so clumsily?

"Are you shopping for something special?" he asked.

"I'm looking for something to wear to the faculty reception. What do you think?" She held the full red skirt away from her hips. That necessitated releasing the bodice, which fell open with a vengeance.

His lips quirked. "I think you'll make quite a splash."

Megan was basking in Tom's approval, thinking that maybe she hadn't forgotten how to flirt after all, when a petite, blond woman appeared at Tom's elbow.

"There you are, Tom. I found what I was looking for." The woman peeked around his shoulder and saw Megan. "It looks like you have, too," she teased.

Tom chuckled as Megan blushed. "Irene Steele, this is Dr. Megan Padget. Megan is chairman of the science department at St. Mark's."

"Ohh." Irene gave the word a wealth of meaning.

Megan wondered if Tom could possibly have mentioned her to his family. How could he? They hadn't even met until today. She was aware of Irene's surreptitious inspection of her, but never guessed what was coming.

"My husband and I are having a cookout tonight, Dr. Padget," Irene said. "Can you join us?"

"Please call me Megan." Megan dearly wanted to spend more time getting to know Tom Steele, but it couldn't be tonight. "I appreciate the invitation, but—"

"It's just a casual family get-together," Irene said in an attempt to head off Megan's refusal.

"I'd love to come, but I already have plans for to-night."

"Oh?" Irene said in a way that asked for an explanation.

Megan didn't want to explain that her activities included providing the centerpieces and dessert for her son's Boy Scout beginning-of-the-year banquet, because she wasn't ready to admit yet that she had a son. She settled for saying, "I made a commitment to...to someone, and I wouldn't feel right breaking it."

Tom had felt a distinct and pleasant relief to discover Megan was unmarried. Now it appeared there was a man in her life, after all. Which was probably just as well, because the woman intrigued him far too much for his own peace of mind.

"I'm sorry to hear that," he said with a shade of irritation in his voice that he wasn't able to control.

"No, I'm the one who's sorry." Megan met Tom's eyes and let her regret show. "Maybe another time."

"Sure," Irene said. "How about next Saturday?"

"You're having another cookout next Saturday?" Megan asked, astonished at having a second invitation issued so promptly.

Irene grinned and laughed, ignoring the way Tom's arm tensed under her hand. "Well, we weren't. But we are now."

Tom was ready to throttle his sister-in-law. It was bad enough that she'd invited Megan once, but the second cookout made her matchmaking attempts too obvious for comfort. It was one thing to buy him a book called *HOW TO MARRY THE WOMAN OF*

YOUR DREAMS. It was quite another to calculatingly invite the woman of his dreams to dinner. He was perfectly capable of doing his own wife hunting, if he wanted a wife. Which he didn't!

"I hope you weren't thinking of including me in that invitation next Saturday," he said, his jaw tight with restrained anger. "I have other plans."

Irene pursed her lips. "Oh, but of course I was. If you can't come..."

Megan saw that Irene was well and truly caught. It was plain she'd only issued the invitation as a way of bringing Tom and her together. Under the circumstances it would be awkward for everybody if she accepted Irene's invitation. Reluctantly Megan said, "I'm afraid I have plans for next Saturday, too. But thanks for the offer."

Hearing Megan was busy the following Saturday as well only confirmed Tom's belief that she was involved with another man. "Are you ready to go, Irene?"

Irene responded to the warning tone in Tom's voice by slipping her arm through his. "Sure. It was nice meeting you, Megan. I'll see you again soon, I hope."

Tom took off with his sister-in-law hanging on to his arm. She turned back to wave and smile as he dragged her away.

Sarah crossed Tom's path on her way back to her mom. "Wow!" she said, staring after him. "Did you see that hunk, Mom? Imagine if you found a guy to marry who looks like that! Think how goggle-eyed the girls would be if I introduced *him* as my new stepfather."

"Looks aren't everything, Sarah. It's more important what kind of person you are."

"Yeah, I know. But he sure looks like he'd be a nice person, doesn't he?"

Megan brushed the bangs away from Sarah's forehead. "You're probably right, honey." Megan had to agree with her daughter's taste in men. Tom Steele was gorgeous; there was no denying it. But she'd meant what she'd said to Sarah. Looks weren't everything. No matter how attracted she was to Tom Steele, and she admitted it was quite a lot, she wasn't going to let herself get emotionally involved with him until she knew whether he was the kind of man who would accept another man's children. She'd met too many men who didn't want a ready-made family.

On the other hand she wasn't willing to tell Tom about Sarah and Chris yet. She wanted to take the time first to find out whether they were compatible as a couple, whether they had interests in common and whether he was the kind of man who could make her laugh, before she took the step of letting him meet her children. She knew her decision was the right one, especially in light of Sarah's adolescent remark about having a stepfather who looked like Tom. It would be infinitely worse if Sarah introduced Tom to all her friends, only to have him disappear when the time came to make a commitment.

Eventually the day of reckoning would come. When it did she was counting on a man as intelligent as Tom had to be to recognize what an asset her two wonderful children were. And if he didn't...well, she had no use for him. None at all.

"Hey, that dress looks really great, Mom. I'll bet any man would take a second look. Are you ready to try on another one?"

The last thing Megan felt like doing was trying on more sexy clothes. But fingering the buttons that lay undone at her throat she admitted that the dress had had an effect. And tomorrow when she showed up at the faculty reception she was determined to finish the job!

Megan spent the rest of Saturday evening after the banquet reading *YOU DON'T HAVE TO STAY SINGLE* and looking for clues as to what she should do and say when she met Tom again on Sunday afternoon. She read the same paragraph over and over.

Be sure to let him do all the talking. Listen to what he says. Make certain you would seriously consider marrying this man before you invest time telling him about yourself.

She felt vindicated in her decision to keep the knowledge of her children to herself. After all, the idea was to vet a man first before revealing everything about yourself. The fact that she was a mother could wait for later meetings when she was sure Tom was real marriage material.

Megan shut her birthday book and placed it on the table beside her bed. She plumped the pillows up behind her and leaned back to think. She'd never really looked on finding a husband as something that could be reduced to cold, calculated planning. She'd fallen in love with Gary in college and had never looked at another man. She hadn't much cared what occupation he chose, how much he liked to talk, how he felt about religion or money. Those were all issues *YOU DON'T HAVE TO STAY SINGLE* had suggested she broach with a prospective husband.

Yet having lived through a not-so-idyllic marriage with Gary she could see how if she'd asked some of those questions in the first place, she and Gary might have been saved a lot of heartache. Once the rosy blush had worn off their marriage, they'd fought constantly about money, about how much time they spent at their respective jobs and even about how many children they should have. Their lack of honest communication had resulted in painful years of isolation and loneliness, and finally in divorce. Marriage wasn't something she would ever wander blindly into again.

She had scoffed at the idea of taking advice from a book on how to find a husband, but so far everything she'd read in *YOU DON'T HAVE TO STAY SINGLE* was proving to be correct. Tomorrow would be another test. She'd ask the questions she was supposed to ask and see how Tom answered. That would tell her whether he was more than a handsome face and a tantalizing body.

Stephanie came to pick her up a little early on Sunday afternoon, and Megan was still dressing.

"Come on into my bedroom, Stephanie," Megan called out. "I'm just about ready."

"Lordy, Lordy! Look at you! What have you got on there? Can that possibly be a garter belt?"

Megan fought a blush. "Advice from page twenty-three. 'Sexy starts from the inside out.' "

"And you shopped for this stuff with Sarah?"

"Uh, not for this. I sent Sarah off with money to buy some jeans while I went to lingerie." Megan pulled on a silk stocking and hooked it to the lacy white garter belt.

"Stand up and let me see you," Stephanie said.

Megan stood and looked at herself in the full-length mirror attached to her closet door. She was wearing a lace bra with insets that revealed a great deal of flesh, but concealed the nipples. Her underwear and garter belt matched her bra in that they "teased," but didn't "go all the way." Megan pulled on a sheer half-slip that was decorated in equally sexy lace, then slipped her dress over her head.

"That dress isn't like anything I've ever seen you wear before," Stephanie said. "It's more..."

"Suggestive?"

Stephanie shook her head. "Not exactly. More like promising. It says come take a look. But it doesn't say touch. Some guy is going to go crazy when he finds all that lace underneath that come-hither dress."

Megan smoothed the clingy white cotton knit over her stomach and hips. She reached up to fasten only two of the six or seven tiny buttons in the front, letting the soft cotton top fall open in a deep V that revealed the shadow between her breasts.

"Boy, when you go to school you learn your lessons well," Stephanie said. "I can't believe the difference a dress makes."

"Then you like it?"

"The question isn't whether I like it. It's whether Tom is going to like it."

"And?"

Stephanie laughed. "He's going to like it."

Megan slipped tiny pearl earrings into her pierced ears, recalling that her book had said:

The less jewelry you wear the better. Remember to keep earrings small so he can see they won't get in his way if he wants to nibble. Don't wear any jewelry that looks like it might have been given to you by another man. That means no rings and no pendant necklaces.

Megan took off the diamond necklace that she'd had made from the engagement ring Gary had given her so many years ago. She really thought this was going too far, but now that she'd committed herself to following the book's advice, she might as well go whole hog.

She slipped into the three-inch taupe heels she'd bought to complement the dress and grabbed a matching clutch purse. "We'd better get going."

The president's house was done in elaborate Spanish-style architecture that was popular in parts of Miami. It had numerous arches, tile floors, stucco walls and wrought iron framing the large windows. There was a tile fountain in the center of the rear patio where most of the faculty had congregated. The backyard bordered on Biscayne Bay and there was a dock where a boat could be moored. Even though the late August day was hot, the breeze off the bay made it seem cooler than it was.

"This is lovely," Megan said to Stephanie, her nose turned into the wind, her hair streaming out behind her. "I'd love to live on the water like this. Wouldn't you?"

"Yes, I would."

Megan turned, somehow not surprised that the voice that had answered her was Tom's and not Stephanie's.

"Your friend went to get some more punch. Can I get you anything?"

"No, I'm fine."

They took a moment just to enjoy looking at one another. Megan couldn't take her eyes off Tom's face. His green eyes sparkled with pleasure, his lips curved with delight, and she knew without having to be told that he admired what he saw. But he didn't leave her to guess what he was thinking.

"You look lovely today." Tom heard the compliment roll off his tongue and knew it was a line he'd used a hundred times with other women. He'd wanted to say something different to Megan. Something special. "You look . . . nice," he told her at last, helpless to speak what he really felt.

"Thank you. You look very nice yourself," she responded.

Tom had donned a pale yellow short-sleeved shirt with a rep stripe tie and form-fitting navy slacks that emphasized his lean waist and flat belly. She fought a smile as she admitted that the view from the front was equally as enticing as the one she'd had from the back at the first faculty meeting. Her gaze caught on one of his muscular forearms, which were covered with a light dusting of black hair. She followed an enlarged vein down his arm to a strong wrist and finally to the large hand that grasped a bottle of beer. The fingers of his other hand caressed the bottle, and Megan shivered at the thought of those hands smoothing along her perspiration-glazed skin.

She looked up into Tom's eyes and knew their physical attraction was mutual. *Looks aren't everything,* she warned herself. It was time to get to the business of finding out more about Tom.

"Is your home in Washington anything like this?" She gestured toward the Spanish mansion.

"No. Everything in my neighborhood is Colonial."

"Which do you like better?"

"I can see how the high ceilings and large windows this house has would be an advantage in a place as warm as Miami. But I have to admit that something draws me to a brick house. Maybe it all goes back to the days when my mother told me the story of the Three Little Pigs."

Megan quirked a brow in bemusement.

Tom groaned inwardly. *You idiot! The Three Little Pigs?!* He ground his teeth. Determined to try to salvage the situation he explained, "The wisest pig had a house of brick. I guess that's why a brick house has always seemed like a smart investment to me."

Megan laughed. "I hope all your economic decisions aren't based on fairy tales."

"Hardly." *Good God, man! Look what you've got her thinking now!* "I admit I have my share of dreams about how I'd spend a fortune if it dropped into my lap."

"Such as?"

For a minute Megan thought he wasn't going to answer her. His gaze skipped out to follow a sailboat on the bay.

"I'd buy a boat and sail around the world," he said.

Megan felt her heart dropping to her shoes. He was a wanderer. A wanderer would make a terrible husband and an even worse father. "Do you do a lot of sailing?" she forced herself to ask.

"Not as much as I'd like. To be honest, I'd be content to sail closer to shore if I just had the time to do it."

Megan breathed a sigh of relief.

Ask her something, Steele. "What about you? What do you dream of, Megan Padget?"

"I guess I'm more the practical type. I try to do the best with what I have, rather than dream about what I can never have."

"It's the dreamers who shape the future," he said.

"It's the practical people who make those dreams a reality," she countered.

Talk with her; don't argue. "I'll concede one is as necessary as the other," he said with a wry smile, "which shows you how much of a politician I've become over the years in D.C."

"I've often wondered—"

"I'm sorry to interrupt," Dean Sawyer said, putting a hand on Megan's shoulder, "but Tom has a call from Washington. It seems there's some emergency—"

"Which phone?" Tom asked.

"You can take it in the president's study. I'll show you the way."

Tom turned to Megan. "Will you excuse me?"

"Of course." What else could she say?

He was gone a moment later. Megan had been amazed at the instant change in Tom's demeanor. His laid-back manner clearly hid an astute advisor. She wondered what other deceptive coloring he'd used to disguise the real Tom Steele.

"Well, do you have a date with Tom?"

Megan hadn't seen Stephanie coming and her friend's hand on her shoulder had startled her so she spilled her wine. "No, I do not have a date with Tom."

Stephanie looked disappointed. "I was sure he would ask you out."

"We were interrupted when he got called away to the phone."

"Maybe he'll be coming back out to find you later."

"Maybe," Megan said. "But I wouldn't count on it."

"What makes you say that?"

Megan shrugged. "I don't know. It's just a feeling I have."

"So where do you go from here?"

"I don't know."

"What's the next chapter in your book?" Stephanie asked.

"I think it's called, 'You *Can* Ask Him Out.' "

"There you have it then. The problem is solved."

"What problem and how is it solved?"

"Why, the problem of how to get Tom to ask you for a date," Stephanie said. "You simply ask him first."

Megan laughed out loud. "You've got to be kidding. I've never asked a man out in my life. And to start with a man like Tom Steele...I just couldn't do it. Besides, in our society it's the man who does the pursuing. It's hardly romantic if the woman has to do the asking."

Stephanie sighed loudly. "Think how great it would be if we could. Of course it's up to you, but I'd think from Tom's point of view, it would be romantic to be asked out by a beautiful woman. I mean, imagine what an awful burden it is for a man to always have to make the first move, to have to be the one to set himself up to be rejected. This way at least he'll know you're interested in him."

"Then I'm the one who's setting herself up for rejection!"

"You've got as much information to go on as he does. Is he interested in you?"

"I think so," Megan replied hesitantly.

"Do you think he thinks you're interested in him?"

"I think so," Megan repeated.

"So what's the problem? If it's custom you're worried about, customs are changing all the time. If the book says it's all right to do it, try it. At least think about it."

"Sure," Megan said. "I'll think about it."

But there was no way on earth she was ever going to come up with the courage to ask Tom Steele out on a date.

Four

The first few weeks of school were always hectic, and Megan didn't even have time to think about Tom Steele, let alone work up the courage to ask him out. But they did cross paths several times on campus. Tom was always cordial, though not particularly talkative. Megan wondered if her intuition had been wrong. Maybe he hadn't been attracted to her after all. Maybe it had been wishful thinking on her part. For a woman who had touted herself as a realist, rather than a dreamer, she was holding on to some pretty farfetched hopes where Tom Steele was concerned.

"Hello there."

At first she thought she'd imagined Tom's voice. But when she looked up she saw that she had very nearly run right into him. She hugged her textbooks closer to her for security. "Hi."

"Fancy meeting you here," he said.

"Yeah, fancy that."

Tom looked at the woman before him and felt a frustration he couldn't voice. Why couldn't he manage to sound like something other than a tongue-tied adolescent whenever he got near her?

"How are your classes going?" she asked.

"Fine," he answered. "How about yours?"

"Fine."

Megan looked at Tom and wondered why it was that their conversations on campus always seemed so stilted. And yet neither of them made any move to leave.

"So, what have you been doing lately?" he went on.

"Not much. And you?"

"Me neither."

They both stood silent a moment until Tom thrust a hand brusquely through his hair, said, "I'll be seeing you around," and stalked off.

This is damned ridiculous, he thought as he pictured the look of confusion on Megan's face when he'd turned tail and run from her. When he reached the sanctuary of his campus office he closed the door and leaned back against it. He was an intelligent, educated, internationally known authority on South American politics. But he could write what he knew about women on the head of a pin. His father hadn't been any kind of role model to follow where behavior with women was concerned, and if Sally hadn't been so persistent during his college years and done most of the talking it was likely they would never have married. Now that he thought about it, Maryanne had done most of the talking, too. It was a miracle he'd managed to get by for so long without anyone ever discovering his secret.

Everyone, men and women both, always assumed that a man like him must have had a lot of experience with women. After all, they assumed, his looks could get him anyone he wanted. Tom shook his head in disgust. It was true he was a good lover. But only because he'd cared enough to take the time to learn how to please the few partners he'd had. He'd said no a lot more times over the years than anyone might suspect. And when he'd been ready to say yes there'd been more than enough willing women eager to fill his needs. He hadn't had to say anything. The women had been glad to do the asking.

This time he wanted to do the pursuing. But it wasn't as simple as he'd thought. Although he wanted to ask Megan out for a date, he couldn't seem to come up with the right words. Hell, to tell the truth, he couldn't seem to come up with *any* words. But for the first time in his life he wanted to do something about it.

His eyes landed on the copy of *HOW TO MARRY THE WOMAN OF YOUR DREAMS*. He'd brought it into the office in case he got bored during the day and needed a laugh. Right now he didn't feel much like laughing. He crossed to his swivel chair, grabbing the book on the way. He leaned back and opened the book to the second chapter, "That First Fabulous Date."

First impressions are everything. You must plan your initial outing with the woman of your dreams very carefully. Try for something original, and make it an event that offers many opportunities to talk.

"In other words, don't take her out to dinner and the movies," Tom murmured aloud. He kept reading, finding the dating suggestions he was certain would be there.

Go to a museum opening.

He always felt a sense of reverence whenever he was in a museum that forced him into silence. He had enough trouble making conversation without that inhibiting factor.

Take a walking tour of the city.

He was sure he would enjoy such a tour, but from what he'd been able to determine, Megan was already familiar with the area. She'd end up carrying the conversation, and that was exactly what he was trying to avoid.

Attend a lecture.

He thought that sounded more promising. He sought out the *Miami Herald* he'd brought with him that morning and paged through the entertainment section to see what he could find. Unfortunately the only two talks being held over the weekend related to South American politics. He'd end up lecturing to Megan before the date was over, and he didn't want that. He went back to his birthday book for another idea.

Go to the zoo.

Tom leaned back in his chair, put his feet up on his desk and laced his hands together behind his head. When was the last time he'd gone to the zoo? Not for years. He'd tried to convince Maryanne to go with him to see the pandas at the National Zoo, but she hadn't been interested.

He picked up the entertainment section of the newspaper again. He thought he remembered seeing an advertisement for the zoo, and sure enough he found it. Miami's Metrozoo boasted a new Australian exhibit that featured koalas. He smiled. Well, they weren't pandas, but they were equally exotic and cuddly looking. He read the rest of the ad, which mentioned there was an outdoor amphitheatre. He and Megan could take a picnic and eat while listening to a popular rock group.

The more Tom read, the more sure he was that he'd stumbled upon the perfect First Fabulous Date. It would be fun, and the antics of the wild animals would hopefully provide lots of conversational material. He sighed with relief. He could see now how his birthday book might have some value after all.

He kept looking to see if the book offered any advice on actually conducting the date. Sure enough, there it was: "Dating Protocol." He grinned. He was an expert on protocol, so this should be a cinch. His grin faded as he kept reading.

Many women today insist on taking their share of the financial burden of dating, and actually disapprove of a man who wants to pay for everything.

Tom's lips pursed thoughtfully. Surely Megan wouldn't expect to pay if he asked her out on a date. Maybe he was old-fashioned, but that was the way he felt. He hadn't thought of himself as a chauvinist, either, but maybe he was. *Or maybe it's just that you have to be in control.*

The flash of insight rocked Tom back in his chair. Was that really why he thought a man had to pay...to stay in control of the situation? He shook his head, unwilling to accept that explanation of his motives. He'd surely gotten past that after losing Sally. Anyway, Megan hadn't struck him as the sort of woman who'd insist on paying her own way. And if she did...

He sighed and admitted that if she did, his beliefs were going to be put to the test.

He forced himself to keep reading, and groaned aloud when he read the last two paragraphs in the chapter.

> *It's important to use your time together to find out whether or not you're compatible. This means asking probing questions and demanding honest answers. Will you still want to be married to this woman in a year? Five years? Twenty-five years? The questions you ask on this First Fabulous Date should be focused to answer these questions.*

He'd never been one for finding out the intimate details of a woman's life. But this book seemed to suggest that the secret to a successful marriage, the key to marrying the right woman in the first place, was as simple as asking questions before you committed yourself. He was just going on a *date* for pete's sake, not to a summit conference! But all the same, he thought of several things it would be nice to know about Megan Padget. Maybe he could just work them casually into the conversation.

Megan was in the kitchen fixing supper when the phone rang. ''Will you get that, Sarah?'' she called to the living room.

''Sure, Mom.''

At that instant it occurred to Megan that it might be Tom on the line—and she hadn't told him she had children. She raced her daughter to the phone, notwithstanding the meat-loaf mixture coating her hands, and caught Sarah just before she lifted the receiver. "I've got it. I just remembered I'm expecting a call." She waited for Sarah to walk away before she picked up the phone, praying it wasn't one of Sarah's many friends, after all.

"Hello. Padget residence."

"Is that you, Megan?"

"Tom. Hello. Yes, it's me." Megan couldn't help the smile on her face, which came out as pleasure in her voice. He'd called. She hadn't realized how much she'd been hoping he would until now.

"Um..."

Megan waited, but when he didn't say anything she asked, "Was there something you wanted to talk with me about, Tom?"

"Yes. I...um..." Tom suddenly had second thoughts about asking Megan to the zoo. Maybe that wasn't the sort of thing women did nowadays. But it was too late to come up with anything else, so he said, "Would you like to go the zoo with me on Saturday?"

"The zoo? Saturday?"

Tom cursed under his breath. For crying out loud! How could he have thought she'd want to go to the zoo? "That is, unless—"

"I'd love to go... Are you still there, Tom?"

"I'm here. That's great. I'll pick you up early, say eight in the morning?"

Megan searched her mind to think of a way she could keep Tom from coming to the house. Sarah was bound to remember him from the department store, and that would lead to speculation by her daughter that could only cause problems if things failed to develop between her and Tom.

"Uh...why don't we meet for breakfast on Saturday?" Megan countered. "I know a lovely Jewish deli that has every kind of fresh bagel your heart desires."

Tom felt a rippling unease about Megan's counterproposal, then shrugged and said, "That sounds good. I'll pick you up—"

"No! I mean, it's on my way to Metrozoo and there's no sense you driving out of *your* way. Nell's is on U.S. 1, south of the city. The exact address is in the phone book. I'll meet you there at 8:00 a.m. sharp on Saturday. Is there anything I can bring?"

"No. I'll take care of lunch," Tom said firmly. "See you on Saturday."

Megan didn't arrive at Nell's until 8:45 a.m. At the last minute Sarah and Chris had gotten into an argument and she hadn't wanted to leave until it was settled. She'd just turned onto I-95 when her left rear tire had gone flat. Megan had never changed a tire so fast in her life. She looked down at the smudges on the clingy pink T-shirt and white shorts that she'd donned this morning to be dressed for *sex*cess. It couldn't be helped. At least she was here. She took a deep, calming breath and let it out. Now if only Tom had waited for her.

Nell's was crowded, as she'd expected it to be. She searched for a familiar set of broad shoulders and a head of wavy black hair, but didn't see them. Her heart sank. A man like Tom Steele probably wasn't used to waiting for a woman. She could hardly blame him. After all, she was forty-five minutes late. Then she spotted him waving at her. She crossed quickly and joined him in a booth at the rear of the deli.

"I'm sorry I'm late," she said breathlessly.

"It was worth the wait." His approval of her attire was clear in his green eyes. "I must admit I've already succumbed to a bagel with my cup of coffee. What would you like?"

"I'll have a cinnamon-raisin one." Megan couldn't believe how understanding he'd been. He hadn't even forced her to resort to excuses, although she felt compelled to explain, "I had a flat tire. That's why I was so late."

"In that case, congratulations for getting here as soon as you did. Did you have any problems getting it changed?"

"I had a little trouble with the lug nuts, but otherwise it was a breeze. I'm afraid I came out a little the worse for wear, though. I—"

"You changed the tire yourself?"

Megan laughed at the astonished look on Tom's face. "Of course. Why wouldn't I? You're not one of those men who thinks a woman should depend on a man for everything, are you?"

Tom took so long answering her question that Megan feared he was going to say he was. She rushed to fill the dead air with, "I'm not a feminist or anything. At least I don't think I am. But I do believe women today have to learn to be self-sufficient. Don't you agree?"

Before Tom could formulate an answer for an issue he'd never confronted in the past, she'd continued, "Although I wish that being self-sufficient didn't sometimes mean having to get dirty." She slid around the curved booth closer to Tom. "Just look at my T-shirt and shorts."

All Tom saw were the long, slender thighs coming out of the shorts, and the pattern of lace in Megan's bra under her T-shirt—which he guessed he could have off her in two seconds flat. He tamped down his libido and said, "I'm glad to see you dressed for the heat. I understand there isn't a lot of shade at the zoo."

"How true. I went there a month or so ago with—" Megan stopped herself just in time from admitting she'd gone to the zoo with her children. "With a friend of mine."

Tom heard the same implication he'd heard before—that Megan was involved with another man. He told himself it didn't matter. She was here today with him, wasn't she? And almost too close for comfort. Her thigh was only inches from his own, and since he'd worn shorts, too, it wouldn't have taken much to press his hard, hairy leg against her soft, smooth one. He reached over for a packet of sweetener for his coffee and edged away slightly. Better to remove temptation altogether.

But he was tempted. More than he cared to admit. He told himself she was just another beautiful woman. After what he'd been through with Sally and Maryanne, he would be crazy to let himself get emotionally involved with her. He would accept what she had to offer physically and that would be that. Anyway, all they were going to do today was enjoy each other's company. This was just a simple date.

"Don't eat too many bagels," he warned. "I've packed us a pretty large lunch."

"Don't worry," Megan said with a grin. "As big as Metrozoo is, we'll walk breakfast off without any problem."

Megan ate quickly. When the waitress brought the check she leaned over to look at it. "Let's see. My half of the bill—"

"I'll get it." Tom lifted the check out of her reach.

"Then I'll leave the tip."

"I said I'll get it."

Megan cocked her head at Tom's curtness. Maybe he was more upset about her lateness than he'd let on. She hoped he wasn't going to let that affect their day. But as soon as he'd paid the check his good humor returned.

"What animals do you want to see most?" he asked as they walked out to his car.

"The ones closest to the main gate," she teased.

Tom laughed.

"You think it's funny now. Let's see how you feel in a couple of hours. That zoo has got *miles* of walkways. I hope you don't mind driving. I've got the spare on one wheel and it's not in very good shape."

Tom was startled again that she'd even considered taking her car. "I invited you. I'll drive."

"Golly, look at this!" she exclaimed when he opened the door to a dark blue, shiny, late-model American sedan. "It looks brand new!"

"I take good care of my car. I'm glad to see it shows."

"It does." She sat carefully on the plush seats so the spots of grease on her shorts didn't touch the upholstery. "It's absolutely immaculate."

Megan was thinking how the exterior of her car hadn't been waxed once in the two years since she'd bought it secondhand with a dent. And how the interior, while uncluttered, had that lived-in look that comes from hauling loads of eight-year-old boys to baseball games and fourteen-year-old girls to cheerleading practice. Their cars were definitely not a compatible facet of their life-styles.

She wondered whether he kept his house as clean as his car. Surely not. But she might as well know now as later. "Are you as conscientious with your house as you are with your car?"

"Hell, no!" He flashed a self-deprecating grin. "I mean, I'm not a total slob at home, but I like things comfortable, and that means accessible. I've got a lady who comes in to clean my place in D.C. I've been looking for someone to do the same here. Do you know anybody?''

"Afraid not," Megan said, a cheerful smile on her face now that she knew that not only didn't he expect an immaculate house but he also was willing to hire a maid to clean. "I do my own housekeeping. But I'll ask around for you."

Megan's earlier words regarding the miles of walkways at the zoo turned out to be more true than Tom could have imagined. Metrozoo had gone beyond steel bars and concrete cages. He and Megan had to literally hike between the enormous natural habitats that had been created for the various species of wild animals.

As they watched some white tigers wind around the East Indian statuary within their area Megan said, "I worked for a boss once who paced like that."

"Oh? A professor?"

"No. I used to be a loan officer with a bank in downtown Miami."

"Why did you quit?"

I got pregnant with Sarah. "Oh, you know how those things go. I needed a change."

"It was fortunate for me that you turned to education."

His voice was low and husky and when Megan looked up into his eyes she saw the warmth of desire. She tried to stay relaxed when Tom slipped his arm around her waist to head her toward the next exhibit.

"Shall we go see the koalas now?" he said. "Although I don't see how they could be any softer than you are."

Megan felt a shiver of excitement course down her spine as Tom's fingers caressed her waist. "The koala exhibit sounds good," she said, her voice breathless. "Let's go."

Tom's arm stayed around her during the entire walk to the koala exhibit, and Megan enjoyed the feel of his tall, male body aligned with hers. Her arm had gotten in the way between them until he'd finally wrapped it around his waist. She could feel the hard muscle beneath the cotton shirt, and she would have given anything if she could have touched his bare skin.

The koalas were so adorable they could have been posing for Australian tourist posters. Tom and Megan spent a lot of time smiling and laughing as they walked from place to place. Despite the advice they'd both received from their respective birthday books, the talk between them stayed trivial, fun—and safe.

Megan was having such a wonderful time she had to remind herself that she was supposed to be vetting Tom as a prospective husband. She racked her mind to think what subjects she ought to cover, and mentally flicked through them: attitudes toward money, goals, needs in a mate...

According to her birthday book, the key to knowing who Tom was lay in the activities and events that had shaped him as a youth. All her questions were supposed to be aimed at his past. Megan felt a twinge of guilt for what she was about to do. However, if she and Tom were incompatible it was important to find that out before they'd spent too much time together. The answers Tom gave her now should tell her a lot about the man he was.

She took a deep breath and asked, "Do your parents live in Miami, too?"

"My father is dead," he said flatly. "My mother has remarried and lives in San Antonio."

She couldn't believe the harshness in Tom's voice. "How old were you when your father died?"

"Fourteen."

Megan could feel the tension radiating from him. This was not a subject she wanted to pursue, but his reaction made her sure it was an important one.

"It must have been awful to lose your father so young."

"On the contrary. His death was a blessing."

Megan stopped and pulled from Tom's embrace to face him. "You can't mean that!"

"Oh, but I do."

"Why?"

His eyes lit with anger as he spoke. "He was an alcoholic. When he was drunk—and I don't even remember him sober—he beat my mother, and when he was done with her he started in on me and my brother."

Megan had no experience with the kind of childhood Tom was describing. She could only empathize with the little boy who'd apparently been brutalized by his father. "I'm sorry. It must have been terrible for you all."

"I've always been afraid I'd turn out like him."

Megan stiffened. "Do you have a drinking problem?"

"Of course not!"

"Have you ever hit a woman?"

"Never! I wouldn't lift a finger—"

"Then why on earth would you compare yourself to your father?" Megan said.

"I know it isn't rational. It just doesn't seem to be something I can control."

Tom was upset that he'd said as much as he had, and even more amazed that he'd said anything at all. "Look, let's talk about something else, shall we?"

Megan slipped her arm back around his waist in an unconscious effort to comfort him and waited until he'd put his arm around her again to start talking. "Did you play any sports in high school?"

"I was one of those tiny ninety-pound weaklings you read about on the back of comic books," he admitted ruefully. "But I ran cross-country for a couple of years."

"I can't imagine you skinny." She eyed his broad shoulders and muscular arms.

"Believe it," he said. "You wouldn't have looked twice at me if you'd seen me in the ninth grade."

"What happened to change you?"

He grinned. "I took the comic book's advice and started lifting weights. In fact, lifting weights and running have both stayed with me to this day."

"Well, may I say they've stood you in good stead?" A twinkle of admiring humor lit Megan's eyes as she ran a hand across his broad chest and patted his flat stomach. She felt him suck in an abdomen that rippled with muscle and her eyes met his, the humor quickly turning to something else. She cleared her throat and looked away from the sensual fire in his green eyes. Sexual attraction was fine when you were considering an affair. However, sex alone was not enough on which to base a marriage. She forced her thoughts to the questions she knew she should be asking.

"So how did a jock like you end up an expert on South American politics?"

"If you really want to know, I'll tell you," he said as they arrived at the amphitheatre. "But why don't we talk over lunch?"

That was easier said than done. The band was louder than Tom had expected, and the conversation he'd hoped for over a lunch of fried chicken, potato salad and fresh fruit was curtailed by the rhythmic pounding of a bass guitar and drums.

Megan was glad for the hiatus in their discussion. She had a lot to think about. Tom's background was not the sort she would have guessed for a man who'd made such a success of himself. It was impossible to imagine him suffering so much physical punishment and emotional abuse as a child, or to imagine him as unattractive as he said he'd been. Supposedly a man's image of himself was formed in adolescence. Did that mean Tom still perceived himself as unwanted? Or, even more unbelievable, that he perceived himself as unattractive to women, despite what must be overwhelming evidence to the contrary any time he looked into the mirror?

"What are you thinking?" Tom asked when there was a break in the music.

What an enigma you are. "How much I'm enjoying your company." She smiled up at him. "What do you think of the band?"

"They're loud."

Megan laughed.

"Let's get out of here," he shouted to her. "This is a little more than I can handle on a full stomach."

As they walked, Megan tried to think of another topic of conversation recommended by her birthday book, mentally listing the ones she'd covered and the ones she hadn't. Ah, yes . . . goals.

"I understand you came to St. Mark's because you could have access to primary South American research materials here in Miami. Are you working on anything special?"

"As a matter of fact, I am. I'm looking for a solution to the current political unrest in Central America."

Megan whistled long and low. "That's a pretty tall order. Is there a solution?"

"That's what I'm going to try to find out. Plain old economics is at the root of a lot of the evils being committed. The rich want to keep what's theirs and the poor want a share of what they haven't got. Each side is attempting to kill off the other to solve the problem. Whether any kind of real social, economic and political reforms can be implemented while there's such a grueling war of attrition going on is debatable.''

Megan chewed on her lower lip as she thought over what he'd said. "So it's a 'which comes first, the chicken or the egg' kind of problem, right? You can't stop the war without reforms, and you can't have reforms while there's a war going on."

"You're very perceptive."

"It's the first time anyone's explained the problem to me in such understandable terms. I hope you do find a solution. What happens when your year here is up?"

"I go back to Washington."

"Would you ever consider staying in Miami?" Megan held her breath for his answer.

Tom linked his arm around her waist and pulled her into the small shade created by a palm tree along the path. He turned to face her, his hands framing her waist, his thumbs nearly meeting at her belly button. "I have to admit it would be nice to live closer to Randy and Irene. But it would mean doing a lot of extra flying to give advice on the Hill. There'd have to be a pretty compelling reason to stay."

How about marriage? she thought.

"What about you?" Tom asked, his thumbs tracing Megan's ribs. "Have you ever wanted to live anywhere else?

Megan struggled to control an involuntary shiver as Tom's thumbs caressed her through the soft cotton T-shirt. "I sometimes dream about living in the mountains out west. Maybe in Colorado or Wyoming or

Montana. At least that's where I take my vacation every year."

"Is there anyone who'd miss you if you left Miami?"

"Uh . . . no."

Tom wanted to make sure once and for all that there was no other man in her life. So he pressed her by asking, "Then there's been no one to take the place of your husband?"

Megan couldn't breathe. Weren't these rather personal questions for a first date? But then she'd been asking some pretty personal questions herself, and she supposed she owed him an honest answer. "I . . . uh . . . haven't exactly been looking for someone to replace Gary."

"Oh? Why not?"

"I guess I should say I did look, but I stopped." *Until my daughter gave me this book. . . .*

"And why was that?"

"I couldn't find anyone who . . . seemed . . . right."

"No? And what were you looking for that you couldn't find?"

His thumbs had tightened on her waist and he applied pressure to her back with his fingers to angle her hips toward him. She kept her eyes focused on the tuft of black hair that showed at the open collar at his throat. Since he wasn't wearing an undershirt she could see that his whole chest was covered with hair. She wanted to thrust her hands into it, to feel the texture of his skin. Unaware that her thoughts showed in her eyes, she met his intense gaze. "Uh, what was that you said?"

Tom exerted great effort to control the heated arousal caused by her glance, and said in a voice that he hoped didn't reveal the extent of his inner turmoil, "I asked what you were looking for in a husband."

"Companionship, for one thing."

"You haven't been able to find a man to keep you company?"

"Not one who..." *Not one who wanted both me and my children.*

"Not one who what?"

"One who was willing to share everything about my life, both the good times and the bad."

He stopped fighting his inclination and pulled her closer, bringing their hips into shocking contact, fitting his hardness to her softness. She cradled him intimately, and he felt the tension as he strove to keep himself still against her. The slight breeze carried the scent of gardenias, which he realized was coming from the woman in his arms. "What else do you—did you—want from a prospective husband?" he demanded, his voice a harsh whisper in her ear.

"A satisfying...physical relationship...is important."

"You mean making love?"

"Yes. Loving. Touching." She grasped his arms, fighting the urge to arch her breasts into his chest.

"What else?"

His voice was low, husky, his lips so close to her ear she could feel his warm breath. She could hardly think for the sensations rocketing through her body. "Someone who loves kids . . . please . . . I can't think with you so close."

But she did nothing to pull away from him.

And he did nothing to separate their bodies.

It was the sound of a little girl calling to her mother that finally broke the spell between them. Megan jerked backward, and the sudden movement caused Tom to release her.

All at once Megan was aware of the heat. Her T-shirt stuck to her skin and her arms and legs felt slick with sweat. She held her top away from her body and shook it a couple of times so the breeze could reach her skin.

"Goodness. It's really too hot to be out here this time of day. Maybe we should check out the aviary. It's like a jungle, cool and dark."

Tom's initial inclination was to demand more answers from Megan. But the truth was, he already knew a great deal more than he'd expected to find out. He'd learned two very important things today. First, that Megan Padget wanted the same things he did from a spouse. And second, that he wanted to know her better.

They spent the rest of the day until dusk walking without doing much talking. Megan was too caught up in the overwhelming response she felt for Tom to carry on an intelligent conversation. The thing that frightened her was the knowledge that she could easily forget all the things she'd learned about Tom's upbringing that might not make him good husband material in favor of the physical satisfaction she was almost certain she would find in his arms.

Megan didn't want the pain that inevitably accompanied a brief sexual fling. She'd gone through that stage when she'd first divorced and found it so unpleasant she hadn't ever had the inclination to repeat her one experience. But with Tom... She found herself looking forward to the end of the day because she hoped he would take her in his arms and kiss her. And Tom didn't disappoint her.

It was nearly dark when they reached Nells. Tom had already learned not to expect her to wait for him to help her out of the car. He quickly caught up to her and placed an arm around her waist to escort her to her car. "I've had a wonderful time today, Megan."

"I have, too," she answered, her voice low and throaty. Megan chastised herself for getting excited over what was probably going to be a goodnight peck on the cheek. But her breathing was already erratic and there wasn't much she could do about it.

Tom didn't intend to do more than touch his lips to Megan's. He left his hand loosely around her waist when he leaned down and brushed her mouth with his. But her lips were soft and sweet, and he went back for another taste. His mouth lingered on hers, and without conscious thought his tongue slipped out to taste the underside of her lip.

He felt his body tensing and fought against it. He lifted his head, his eyes hooded, his breathing harsh. But at the sight of Megan's mouth, glistening with moisture from his tongue, he lowered his head again,

his other arm going around her as well, drawing her
into the V created by his wide-spread legs. Although
he pulled her tightly into his embrace, his lips were
gentle, seeking.

Megan opened to him like a flower to a spring rain.
He felt his heart go wild, felt his blood start rushing.
His mouth slanted urgently against hers, and she met
his lips eagerly. He used his teeth, nipping at her lip,
then soothed the hurt with his tongue. Eventually his
tongue slid deep inside her mouth. From that instant
he was lost in a vortex of pleasure. His hands roamed
her body as his lips and tongue plundered her mouth.
And yet he wasn't taking, he was giving.

He heard the purr in Megan's throat and groaned in
response. He grasped her buttocks with his hands and
arched her against him, his tongue miming the move-
ments of long-time lovers. He had her T-shirt half-off
when the sound of raucous laughter and the slam of a
car door brought him abruptly from the well of passion into which he'd fallen. He realized they were
standing in the middle of a parking lot.

He tried to speak, but his voice was too hoarse. He
cleared his throat and said, "I'll follow you home to
make sure you get there safely."

For obvious reasons, none of which she could explain to Tom, Megan couldn't let him do that.
"There's really no need." She turned quickly and ran
to her car.

"Wait. I—"

Megan couldn't afford to take the chance he'd follow her. She waved out the window as she backed from her slot.

"See you next week!" she yelled as she shot by him.

Tom stood watching her with his hands balled in fists by his sides. His body was throbbing with need. He was so hard he hurt, and he'd only intended to kiss her goodnight. What had happened? How had things gone awry? *How had he so completely lost control?*

He turned and walked toward his car, stunned to realize how strongly he'd responded to Megan's sensual allure. He'd broken a promise he'd made to himself at fourteen, not to ever allow his emotions free rein. If he could so easily lose himself with this woman with a mere kiss, what might he do when they finally made love? The discussion he'd had with Megan was little comfort. He'd never yet been violent like his father, but then he'd never let himself lose control with a woman, either. The thought was chilling—frightening rather than exciting. The safe course of action— the only sane course of action—was clear to him.

Stay away from Megan Padget.

Five

Her Book: "You *Can* Ask Him Out!"

Megan hadn't seen or heard from Dr. Thomas Steele for weeks. She knew that was partially due to the fact that he'd been called to Washington. But she could find no explanation for the fact that she hadn't even seen him on campus upon his return, except that he didn't want to see her. Like a lovesick teenager she'd waited by the phone night and day for Tom to call. She'd replayed every moment of their date in her head, trying to remember if she'd said anything, or done anything, that might have caused him to avoid her. But nothing came to mind. She hadn't even told him she had two kids! She'd followed her birthday book's advice down to the last comma and period, apparently to no avail.

This morning she'd finally accepted that he wasn't ever going to call. Disillusioned, disgusted and distressed, she'd tossed *YOU DON'T HAVE TO STAY SINGLE* into the trash.

"It's like he disappeared from the face of the earth," she said to Stephanie as they walked through the faculty dining hall line together.

Stephanie grimaced as she slid a soggy burrito onto her plate. "You'd think with a man named Ramon Gonzales in charge of food services here the Mexican cuisine would be a little better."

"Ramon is Cuban."

"That explains everything."

"Have you heard a word I've said about Tom?" Megan asked.

"Sure. You had one wonderful date—including a devastating goodnight kiss—and you haven't seen or heard from him since. You could always call him, you know."

"Call him?"

"Yeah, you know, pick up the phone, dial seven numbers, wait for the ring and when he answers say, 'Hello, this is Megan Padget. I'm dying to jump your bones. Why the hell haven't you called me?'"

Megan laughed. "You're crazy. You know that?"

"Of course. That's why you like me so much." Stephanie heaped her plate with an unappetizing mixture of string beans, onion rings and mushroom sauce. "I'm not kidding. I think you should call him."

"Women don't call men."

"Are we back to that again? This is the eighties. Of course women call men. We call them jerks. We call them slobs. We call them—"

"Enough! Enough! You're no help at all."

"I've given you my best advice. If you choose not to take it, what can I say? Does that birthday book your kids gave you have anything in it to cover this situation?"

"I threw it in the trash this morning."

"That's wasteful. The least you could have done was send it back for a refund."

Megan snorted inelegantly.

"Well, before you threw it out, did you read anything in it that covered this situation?"

Megan gnawed her lip for a moment before she admitted, "Yes."

"Well?"

"It says that this is the eighties and I should call him."

Stephanie chuckled. "Look, what have you got to lose? All he can say is that he never wants to see you again."

Stephanie turned to her friend to see if she'd appreciated her wit only to find Megan's face white, her eyes bleak. Stephanie set her tray down on the closest table and turned to slip an arm around Megan's shoulder. "Hey, you really have got it bad, haven't you? Sit down. We need to talk."

Stephanie maneuvered the two of them to an isolated corner of the dining room. "Now, tell Mama

Stephanie. I've seen lovesick before, but this is ridiculous."

"I've never felt like this before, Stephanie, ever. Not even when I was sixteen and Jimmy Storey gave me his letter jacket. I've been absolutely obsessed with thoughts of this man. I go to sleep thinking about him, I dream about him and he's the first thing on my mind in the morning. I don't like it," she said, biting off the words in anger. "It isn't normal. All the time there's this awful tightness inside. If this is love then you can have it! It hurts. It isn't comfortable. It's damned frightening."

"I can understand it hurts, and it's uncomfortable," Stephanie said. "But frightening? How so?"

Megan closed her eyes and folded her hands together in her lap, feeling again the tension that had her sleeping with her shoulders hunched tensely every night. "I'm afraid that it really is all over. That I'll never see him again."

"I see. Well, then, you don't have a choice then, do you? You'll have to do it."

"Do what?"

"Call up Tom Steele."

Tom was miserable and he had no one to blame but himself. He leaned back in the corduroy chair in his living room and put his feet up on the ottoman. Dusk had come, but he hadn't turned on the lights. He liked it better in the dark. He didn't have to acknowledge that the room was empty...as empty as his life. He laid his hand on the phone that he'd perched on the broad arm of the chair.

Call her, you jerk. So what if you lost control. It was a temporary situation. Now that you know what happened you won't have the same problem.

He snickered. He was just kidding himself. He ached for her now and he hadn't seen her for weeks. And speaking of that, how was he going to explain the fact he hadn't called? He didn't like feeling vulnerable. He didn't like feeling out of control. But he also didn't like the feeling of loneliness that was pervading his life. Maybe it was time to let go of the past. Maybe it was time to take a chance and let himself lose control. Maybe Megan was right, and he really wasn't like his father.

He picked up the phone, dialed three numbers and slammed it down again.

What if she said no?

If you won't take a chance you'll never find a wife. Besides, could the pain of rejection be any worse than what you're already feeling?

He sighed. The past few weeks had been hell. He'd seen Megan on campus several times, but had always managed to avoid her. He supposed he wasn't acting like the typical macho hero in the movies. Those guys always went after the woman they wanted and everything else be damned. It was humbling to admit that he was an ordinary man whose only resemblance to those heroic characters was his looks. They were cardboard characters. He was flesh and blood. His pain was real . . . but so was his need.

Call her.

He took a deep breath and exhaled.

All right. I will.

The jangle of the ringing phone pierced the quiet of the small living room and startled Tom so much that he knocked the phone off the arm of the chair. The receiver went flying and he grappled around in the dark searching for it. When he finally found it, his voice revealed his irritation.

"Hello. Who is it?"

"Tom?"

"Megan?"

The phone was silent for so long Tom thought he must have imagined her voice. "Megan?"

"Yes. Hello, Tom. How have you been?"

"Fine." *Damn! Think of something to say!* "How are you?"

"Fine."

"Uh...look, Megan, I've been meaning—"

"Wait! Before you say anything I want to ask you something."

"Sure. Anything."

Megan swallowed over the lump in her throat, held her hand over a heart that was threatening to burst, it was beating so hard and forced herself to speak calmly. Even so, she choked on her first attempt to speak. She swallowed and tried again. "I...I wondered if you'd like to go to a Halloween party with me. On Halloween. Uh, it's on Saturday night this year, you know."

"I know." Tom was smiling. He couldn't help himself.

"Uh . . . well . . . will you?"

"Yes."

Megan felt her heart thumping madly under her trembling hand. She closed her eyes to fight the dizziness that threatened. "Uh . . . I'll call you later with the details. Think about what costume you want to wear and maybe we can come up with something that matches. All right?"

"Sure."

"Goodbye, Tom."

"Goodbye, Megan."

When Tom heard the phone click at Megan's end he flicked on the lamp, found his phone and set the receiver back in the cradle. Megan had asked him out on a date. And this time he would do things right. He would— Good grief, what kind of protocol applied when the woman asked the man out? Would she let him pay? Should he offer to drive? Should he invite her back to his apartment, or wait for her to invite him to her home? And what if she didn't?

He searched through the stack of papers on the spooled table looking for *HOW TO MARRY THE WOMAN OF YOUR DREAMS*. What the hell had he done with it? It suddenly dawned on him. He'd thrown it in the garbage yesterday! Would it still be there?

He scrambled out of his chair so fast it scraped six inches backward. He stumbled over the spooled coffee table and banged his hip on the edge of the dining-room table on his way out. What day was garbage pickup?

Please be there.

He jerked the lid off the trash can, which was illuminated by a streetlight in the alley. There it was. Right on top. *HOW TO MARRY THE WOMAN OF YOUR DREAMS.* He tenderly rescued it from its place on a pile of old newspapers and tucked it under his arm. Once back inside, he turned on every light in the house, settled into the corduroy chair and opened the book. There was bound to be something in here to cover his date with Megan.

Several hours later he set the book down on the coffee table and rubbed his eyes with the heels of his hands. He'd found nothing that was the least bit helpful regarding dating protocol when the woman asked the man out, except the statement that this occurred occasionally, and it was the lucky man who found a woman smart enough to know her own mind and courageous enough to take the risk of rejection on her shoulders. And what lovely shoulders they were, Tom mused. Thanks to a short excursion into the chapter, "Sex—When to Make Your Move," he hoped to see those shoulders quite soon.

Megan felt the devil dancing in her stomach. Any moment Tom Steele was going to arrive at her door for their second date. She had her best friend and her daughter to thank for this. The same day she'd spoken to Stephanie she'd come home to find Sarah waiting for her at the door with *YOU DON'T HAVE TO STAY SINGLE* gripped tightly in her hand.

"Look what I found in the trash." Sarah's voice had quivered with hurt. "Don't you want to find a husband? Don't you want to get married?"

"Sweetheart, it's more complicated than you think."

"You didn't even try! You didn't even give it a chance!"

Since she hadn't told Sarah about her date with Tom she had no comeback for her daughter's accusation.

"If I gave up this quickly on my homework I'd get a two-hour lecture from you," Sarah had railed.

"It's not the same," Megan had countered.

"What makes this situation any different? You have to keep trying. You have to make an effort. Nobody said it was going to be easy. Does any of that sound familiar?"

It was the beginning of the lecture Megan had given Sarah when her daughter had been stumped by a new math concept.

Sarah thrust *YOU DON'T HAVE TO STAY SINGLE* toward her mother. "It wasn't only for mine and Chris's sake, you know, that we bought this book. It was for your sake, too. Sometimes I see you look at another couple, like when we're in line at the movies and some guy will hug his girl and give her a kiss, and you . . . you look so lonely, Mom. I don't want you to be lonely anymore."

"Oh, Sarah." Megan had held her arms out and Sarah had flown into her embrace. She'd hugged her

NO COST! NO OBLIGATION TO BUY! NO PURCHASE NECESSARY!

PLAY "LUCKY 7" AND GET AS MANY AS SIX FREE GIFTS...

HOW TO PLAY:

1. With a coin, carefully scratch off the silver box at the right. This makes you eligible to receive one or more free books, and possibly other gifts, depending on what is revealed beneath the scratch-off area.

2. You'll receive brand-new Silhouette Desire® novels. When you return this card, we'll send you the books and gifts you qualify for *absolutely free*!

3. Unless you tell us otherwise, every month we'll send you 6 additional novels to read and enjoy. If you decide to keep them, you'll pay only $2.24* per book—that's 26¢ less per book than the cover price! There is *no* charge for shipping and handling. There are no hidden extras.

4. When you subscribe to Silhouette Books, we'll also send you additional free gifts from time to time, as well as our newsletter.

5. You must be completely satisfied. You may cancel at any time simply by writing "cancel" on your statement or returning a shipment of books to us at our cost.

*Terms and prices subject to change without notice.

You'll love your elegant bracelet watch—
this classic LCD Quartz Watch is a perfect
expression of your style and good taste—
and it is yours FREE as an added thanks for
giving our Reader Service a try.

PLAY "LUCKY 7"

Just scratch off the silver box with a coin.
Then check below to see which gifts you get.

YES! I have scratched off the silver box. Please send me all the
gifts for which I qualify. I understand I am under no obligation
to purchase any books, as explained on the opposite page.

225 CIS JAYX

NAME

ADDRESS   APT

CITY   STATE   ZIP

7 7 7	WORTH FOUR FREE BOOKS. FREE BRACELET WATCH AND MYSTERY BONUS
🍒 🍒 🍒	WORTH FOUR FREE BOOKS AND MYSTERY BONUS
⚫ ⚫ ⚫	WORTH FOUR FREE BOOKS
🔔 🔔 🍒	WORTH TWO FREE BOOKS

DETACH AND MAIL CARD TODAY

DETACH AND MAIL CARD TODAY

BUSINESS REPLY CARD

First Class   Permit No. 717   Buffalo, NY

Postage will be paid by addressee

SILHOUETTE BOOKS®
901 Fuhrmann Blvd.,
P.O. Box 1867
Buffalo, NY 14240-9952

NO POSTAGE
NECESSARY
IF MAILED
IN THE
UNITED STATES

daughter hard as she'd fought the sob rising in her throat. She'd pushed Sarah away and said, "Give me that book. I'm going to do something about this right now."

That very evening she'd called to ask Tom Steele out on a date. And he'd accepted.

"What's he look like?" Sarah had asked, when Megan had admitted she had a date for the church Halloween party.

"Do you remember that hunk you saw when I went shopping for clothes?"

"Sure. How could I forget him? Is your date that good-looking, Mom?"

"That's the man I have a date with."

"You're kidding!"

"No, I'm not."

"But Mom, he's a real hunk!"

Megan didn't know whether to feel insulted or not. "And what makes you think I couldn't attract a hunk?"

Sarah had grinned. "I didn't mean it that way. Or if I did, I take it back. You deserve a hunk. Wait until the girls hear—"

"Sarah, I'd rather you didn't say anything to any of your friends just yet."

"Why not?"

"We're just going out on a date, Sarah. It may not come to anything."

"But—"

"No buts. Promise me you won't say anything just yet."

"All right, Mom. Golly, I can't believe this. This is too much. I gotta go write all this down in my diary."

Megan knew she'd taken a chance telling Sarah about Tom. Tonight she was going to take another chance and tell Tom about her children. If the existence of Sarah and Chris was going to be a problem for him, she needed to know it. She'd suggested he pick her up here at the house thinking that would be the easiest way to break the news, but as it turned out, both children were spending the night with friends. In retrospect she was glad she'd be able to pick the moment to tell Tom she was a mother.

The sound of the doorbell startled Megan from her reverie. When she opened the door Tom stood before her dressed in the tailored black suit and white clerical collar of a priest. He looked divine, all right, but in a strictly earthly way. She couldn't take her eyes off him.

"May I come in?"

"Oh, I'm sorry," Megan said. "Please do. I'm nearly ready. I just have to get my cape."

Megan was self-conscious about her outfit, which was a form-fitting, sequined, red devil costume that just happened to zip down the front to a spot somewhere below her belly button. She swirled the black cape around her, trying to arrange it on her shoulders.

"Let me help." Tom came up behind her and adjusted the padded shoulders of the cape and the high, stiff collar that framed her face. She'd put her hair up in a knot on her head, leaving wisps trailing down her neck and at her temples. A headband held two red horns in place. Leaving his hands resting on her shoulders, Tom leaned down and kissed her cheek.

"May I say you look devilishly lovely tonight," he said with a chuckle.

"If I may say you look 'holy' delightful!"

Tom groaned. "That was awful."

"It was, wasn't it?" Megan said, unrepentant. "I must say I'm impressed with your ingenuity. When I said I'd be coming as a devil it never occurred to me that you'd dress as a priest."

"What did you expect?"

"I don't know. Something equally satanic, I suppose. There's a certain irony in us showing up together like this at a *church*-sponsored Halloween party that I don't even want to think about."

For a moment Megan stared up at him, a silly grin on her face. But as he lowered his head again, the grin faded. When his mouth was only an inch away from hers, he paused.

"Megan?"

He was giving her a chance to say no. But Megan was equally tempted and didn't want to be saved. She turned her face up and stood on tiptoe, meeting his mouth and pressing her lips against his, which were firm and unyielding for a moment, but only a moment. As their lips met, her mouth opened to his searching tongue. His arms reached out to pull her into his embrace. Megan was lost in a euphoric daze. Her whole body trembled with excitement. It was their first kiss all over again. The last time this had happened he'd stolen her senses and disappeared from her life . . . and she still didn't know why.

She felt her knees giving way and struggled against the haze of pleasure. When she pulled her mouth away Tom immediately sought out the racing pulse at her throat with his mouth as his hands moved over her rib cage and upward toward her breasts.

"Tom! Please!" She wasn't sure whether she was asking him to stop, or go on. She grabbed his wrists in an attempt to hold his hands in place below her breasts. But her strength wasn't enough to keep him from reaching his goal. She gasped as his hands cupped her breasts, his thumbs caressing the tips, which immediately hardened under his touch. She could feel herself succumbing to his tender persuasion. She was lost . . . unless she could somehow reach him with words.

"Tom, please . . . stop."

The sound of Megan's distraught voice shook Tom from the spell that had gripped him.

"Megan? . . ." He rested his forehead against hers and sucked in several breaths of air, trying to regain his composure.

"Oh, Tom, what makes this happen between us?" she whispered. "I don't understand. . . . When you touch me I . . . can't resist."

He lifted his head and when he saw where his hands were, he jerked them away from her body and staggered backward. He thrust his fingers through his hair leaving it rumpled and wild-looking. "I don't . . . I can't . . ." He ground his teeth together. How could he explain what had happened? He'd been completely out of control. He'd hoped this couldn't happen again. What was it about this woman that caused him to lose all sense of time and place when he held her in his arms?

"Are you all right?" she asked.

"I'm the one who should be asking that, I think," he said with a rueful grimace.

"We should have expected it."

"Oh?"

Megan smiled tentatively. "Look at the costumes we chose to wear. It's a wonder we weren't struck by lightning when we kissed."

Tom managed a chuckle. "I don't know about you, but I think I was."

"Maybe we'd better get to the church party. It'll be safer there."

"For whom?" he said, a grin coming back to his face now that it was apparent Megan was going to give him another chance to show that he could act civilized in her presence. "You're dressed as Lucifer, if I'm not mistaken. That could mean we're in for a hellish evening."

Megan took a step toward Tom, then reached out and slowly entwined her fingers with his. "I happen to believe in a very forgiving God."

"Damned good thing," he muttered as they stepped out the door and into the dark night together.

The church party was being held at Viscaya, an Italian Renaissance-style villa that had been turned into a museum. Tables loaded down with fresh fruit and cheese hors d'oeuvres had been set up outside on the patio that bordered Biscayne Bay. A band was playing golden oldies and gondola rides were being offered for those who chose to take them.

Megan had been a little nervous about how Tom would react when she paid for the tickets, since he'd seemed reluctant to let her use her own money on their first date. However, he said nothing when she handed over her check to Mary Beth Prescott at the table that had been set up for dispensing tickets. Mary Beth, unfortunately, wasn't equally discreet.

"Why, Megan Padget, this is the first man I've seen you with in two years. I must say the wait was worthwhile. Introduce me to the padre."

Furious that Mary Beth would reveal such a thing, even if it was the truth, Megan replied, "This is Father Steele. Father, this is our church secretary, Mary Beth Prescott."

"You mean you're not wearing a costume? You're really a priest?" Mary Beth demanded, shocked.

Tom winked. "What do you think?"

"If it isn't a costume, I think it's a crying shame," Mary Beth said, laughing good-naturedly.

Megan grabbed Tom's hand and hauled him away. "You keep listening to Mary Beth and you're going to get a swelled head." They walked through the crowd and ended up on the stone steps that led to the water. Megan sat and pulled Tom down beside her. "I can't believe how lucky we were with the weather. It's warm tonight, but thanks to the breeze off the bay, not too warm. And the moon is so big and bright we hardly need the paper lanterns.''

Megan realized Tom's attention was elsewhere. She followed his gaze to a woman who was wearing a harem costume. ''It looks like she forgot a few of her seven veils.''

''What? Oh.'' Tom flushed. ''Sorry. I was wondering how someone could wear an outfit like that to a church party.''

Megan laughed. ''We only sponsored the party. It's open to the public. We're trying to earn some money to help support our new family-counseling center.''

She found her own attention wandering as she spied a man wearing a safari outfit, who had a live parrot on his shoulder. ''I recognize him!'' she said with a squeal of delight. ''He's one of the professors at St. Mark's.''

Tom felt himself bristling with antagonism until he noticed that the man Megan had been so delighted to see had his arm around a woman dressed as a French maid. He forced himself to relax, uncomfortably aware that he was exhibiting all the classic signs of a jealous male. Jealousy was an emotion he hadn't experienced in the past, and one with which he had no desire to become familiar. ''Would you like something to drink?''

''Yes. I'll go with you. If we get separated in this crowd we'll never find each other again.''

That made as good an excuse as any to slip her arm around Tom's waist, and Megan took it. She'd never been jealous before, but she recognized the symptoms in herself. As they stood in line at the cash bar

Megan tried to figure out what was causing the feeling. Possessiveness, for one thing. Had she ever felt possessive of Gary? Yes, but there was something else that was needed for jealousy to exist. Distrust. She had no reason to distrust Tom, no reason to believe he would seek out another woman while he was with her. But the problem wasn't with Tom. It was with the extraordinary good looks that caused women to approach him, whether he wished them to do so or not.

Megan examined Tom's chiseled profile. Could she spend a lifetime with a man whom other women found fascinating? Even if she could believe enough in his love to think he would never look at another woman, could she trust other women not to put irresistible temptation in his path? He was only human, after all. Her eyes dropped to the collar at his throat. His saintly appearance was just a costume. All men could be tempted.

She touched Tom's cheek with her fingertips and he turned to look down at her.

"It won't be long now," he said. "Getting thirsty?"

"A little." She reached out to a nearby buffet table and picked up a fresh strawberry. She took a bite from it and felt the juice on her lips. She watched Tom's eyes darken as she licked the juice away. Then she held the berry up to his lips. "Take a bite. It's delicious."

He bit off the berry so his teeth and lips nipped her fingers. She dropped the leafy stem in surprise. "Oh."

"Did I hurt you?" He took her hand in his and brought her fingertips to his lips, kissing them softly. "I didn't mean to."

She pulled her hand from his, shaken by how quickly she'd become aroused. "We're next."

"What would you like?" he asked, his voice husky.

"Bourbon. A double."

He looked at her in surprise, but when she didn't change her mind he ordered it for her, and a beer for himself. When she reached for the money she'd tucked in a small pocket in her outfit he put a hand to stop her.

"I've got it. Are you sure you want this?" he asked as he handed her the double bourbon.

"Yes." She knew she needed something to rouse her from the sexual spell that had been cast. She took a large swallow of the drink, coughing and sputtering when the fiery liquid hit her throat. "God, that's awful!"

"Why did you order it then?"

Megan laughed, a slightly hysterical sound. *I needed something to shock me to my senses.* "I thought it would taste better than it does."

"Would you like to dance?"

Megan looked up at Tom for a moment, wondering how wise it would be to put herself in his embrace. She took another swallow of the bourbon, coughed again and said, "Sure. Why not?"

Tom set his plastic cup of beer on a stone ledge and Megan put her drink beside it.

"Come on." He placed his hand on the small of her back to head her in the right direction. He followed her back up the stairs to the patio just outside the villa and took her in his arms. As they began a slow dance their bodies melded together from breasts to thighs.

"Oh, Lord," Megan mumbled. "I knew it."

"Knew what?" he whispered in her ear.

"That it would feel like this."

Tom didn't reply, merely pulled her closer into his arms, tucking her head against his shoulder, leaning his head down close to hers so he could enjoy the scent of gardenias in her hair.

Neither of them spoke again for the next hour until the band took its break. Megan hardly knew where she was when she felt Tom's hands on her shoulders.

"Megan. The music's stopped."

She looked up into Tom's slightly hooded eyes and knew he was as aroused as she was. It was a pleasant feeling, one of expectation, of anticipation.

"What time is it?" she asked.

"Time to take a walk."

Megan didn't protest when Tom linked their arms and led her away from the villa into the intricate formal gardens. There were other couples wandering the stone pathways, but Tom found a shadowy arbor that was isolated from the noise of the crowd and turned her into his arms.

"Megan, I need you."

His lips claimed hers fiercely, passionately, and Megan willingly opened her mouth to his plundering tongue. His hands skimmed down her back and captured her hips, pulling them into the waiting cradle created by his widespread legs. She could feel the hard length of him, aroused, ready, with only two thin layers of cloth separating their eager bodies. One of his hands grasped her buttocks while the other laid claim to her breasts—first freeing them by making use of the zipper down the front of her form-fitting costume.

Megan arched upward as she felt Tom's warm, wet mouth replace his hand on her breast. Her fingers reached up to clutch his hair.

At that moment the sound of female voices intruded on their idyll. Both Tom and Megan stiffened in the darkness.

"Did you see that man with Megan tonight?"

"Some kind of body on him, huh? His face isn't half-bad, either!"

"You're telling me. I'd like to catch him on one of these paths."

"Good luck beating me to him! She's gotta leave him alone sometime tonight. And then..."

The other woman's drunken giggle made Megan shudder. Her breath rasped in her throat as she shoved her face into Tom's shoulder.

Jealousy. It burned like a fire inside her.

Her hands slipped from Tom's hair and clutched the front of her costume together. She struggled to pull the zipper back up, but it was stuck.

"Help me!" she whispered, resisting the urge to say anything more until she was clothed again and could escape Tom's embrace.

Tom lifted her hands away from the garment and slowly eased the zipper upward. He knew Megan couldn't have helped overhearing the two women.

"They were just making talk. It didn't mean anything."

With the zipper back in place, Megan turned her back on Tom and walked a few steps away from him, giving her racing pulse a chance to slow down. "Are you saying strange women don't make passes at you?"

"Not as often as you seem to think," he said, his voice brusque.

She turned to look at him, but his face was hidden in the shadows. She took a deep breath. "I'm sorry. It's just . . . what they said bothered me."

"I figured as much."

"You might be tempted—"

"I'm not interested in another woman, Megan. I want you. Only you."

He'd taken two steps toward her, and Megan could feel the tension radiating from him. "But what if—"

Tom's mouth came down on hers in a searing kiss that cut her off and left no doubt in her mind that she was the one he wanted. When he finally released her she had to hang on to him to keep from falling.

"I think it's time to leave," she managed to say.

"If that's what you want."

"It's what I want."

She needed time to think, and she couldn't do it this close to Tom. It wasn't until they were driving back up I-95 that Megan realized she'd never told Tom she had children. She wasn't sure how to broach the subject. Finally she said, "Have you ever thought about having children?"

He turned to look at her briefly. He opened his mouth to tell her about his son, but the whole subject was too painful... and ironic. He was the one who'd wanted children and yet it was Sally who'd taken Todd when they'd divorced—taken him across the country to California, where it was difficult, if not impossible to visit him.

He turned back to Megan, unaware of the ferocious scowl on his face. "I always wanted kids. A son who looked like me, and a daughter who..." He forced his thoughts away from the painful past and said curtly, "It was Sally who didn't want children."

"Sally?"

"She was my wife. I'm divorced. I thought you knew."

"I did."

Megan was devastated by what she'd just found out. *A son who looked like me.* She could never give him that. She was glad now that she hadn't introduced him to Sarah and Chris. Because unless he changed his mind about wanting children, it would be fruitless to see Tom Steele again.

Six

His Book: "Sex—When to Make Your Move"
Her Book: "Sex—Don't Jump the Gun"

Aren't you going to invite me in?" Tom asked.

"No."

"Why not?"

"You know why not." Megan put a hand on Tom's chest to keep him from stepping over the threshold. "All we have to do is touch one another and neither one of us can think straight."

"Is that so bad?"

Tom's lazy grin stole Megan's breath. She thought back to the chapter in *YOU DON'T HAVE TO STAY SINGLE* entitled, "Sex—Don't Jump the Gun."

A man judges a woman by how quickly she joins him in bed. No matter how urgently he insists he'll respect her in the morning if she succumbs to their mutual desire—he won't. So think first, and make love only when the time is right for such a commitment.

This was only her second date with Tom and the temptation to let things happen between them was strong. In fact, she knew that if they'd been anywhere near a bed on their first date they'd have landed in it.

Megan felt sure that tonight was too soon to take such a step. There were a lot of issues yet to be settled between them before they were ready to move their relationship any closer to commitment, not the least of which was the existence of her two children and the fact she couldn't give Tom any more.

"Please, Tom, I'm very tired." It was an excuse, and she knew he knew it. Still, she hoped he would accept it.

Tom couldn't help recalling the words in the chapter of his birthday book entitled, "Sex—When To Make Your Move."

It's not always easy to judge when a woman is ready to include sex in your relationship. There are times when she'll say no and mean it. Learn to recognize the signs of such a refusal. She'll resist your touch, and stiffen in response to any physical contact with you.

He put his arms on Megan's shoulders and felt her whole body arch toward him. No resistance there....

On the other hand, there are women who want a man to take the sexual initiative. They will say no and wait for the man to make further overtures to which they willingly respond.

Tom leaned into Megan, pressing her back against the door. He felt a jolt when his hips came into contact with hers, his body hardening in instantaneous response to her heat. When she voiced no protest to his touch, he bent his head, searching for her mouth. He nibbled at her lips, tasting the soft skin with his tongue and teeth.

Megan began to panic. She could feel what little resistance she had to Tom eroding as he began his gentle assault on her mouth, his hips pressing intimately into hers. She had to find a way to distract him.

"Would you like a cup of coffee?" she asked.

Tom lifted his head only slightly. "Would you?"

"Uh ... I guess I'd like something cold."

"Something hot and something cold. Sounds good to me," he murmured in her ear.

Megan shivered with desire as she groped for the doorknob. "Let's go inside, shall we?"

It was dark inside. Megan reached for a light switch, but Tom's hand was there to stop her.

"We don't need the light."

"But your coffee—"

"Did you really invite me in here to have a cup of coffee, Megan?"

His mouth was on her throat, his tongue bathing the racing pulse over which she had no control.

Tom shut the door behind them with his foot, leaving them with only the light from the moon streaming in the front picture window.

"Where's your bedroom, Megan?"

"Tom, it's too soon to—"

"Too soon for this?" His hands were on her breasts, kneading them, his thumbs skimming the tips, bringing them to hardness.

Megan moaned and Tom caught the sound with his mouth. She returned his kiss urgently, feeling caught up in a spiral of desire that had nothing to do with thinking or being sensible.

She felt Tom lifting her to bring her body in line with his need. She could feel the hard ridge pressing into her abdomen and arched her body closer.

"Ahh, Megan, I want you."

"And I want you," she breathed in reply. With the last shred of sanity she had left she tried once more to stop their heedless rush toward ecstasy. "It's too soon, Tom. There's so much we don't know about each other—"

"I know everything I need to know."

Somehow the zipper on her costume was down again and Megan felt the heat and wetness of Tom's mouth and tongue on her breast. He was sucking, drawing the nipple into his mouth to play with it.

"Oh, my God," she moaned. "Tom, we can't...."

But it was only her mind saying no; her body was screaming *yes!* at the top of its lungs.

His hand reached down inside the zipper to stroke the soft skin of her belly and then he reached farther to touch the core of her.

Megan jerked as he reached the sensitive nub, and her hand automatically grasped at his wrist to stop him.

"Too rough?" he questioned, his voice harsh with need. "I'll be more careful."

He touched again, his callused fingertips gently abrading, teasing, taunting, dipping inside her to touch the wetness and then returning to caress the heat and heart of her, building the tension, driving her wild. She could feel her body tautening, feel the urgent pull inside her, and recognized it for what it was. And she wanted it. She wanted what he could give her. So, though she knew she should stop him, she grasped his shoulders with her hands to keep from falling and used her mouth to give him back what pleasure she could. She kissed his neck, his ears, his chin, biting and nipping and sucking, loving the taste of him.

She heard herself groan with pleasure, and needing something to hang onto, she clamped down with her teeth on Tom's shoulder. She cried out again in fulfillment as the tension erupted throughout her body in waves of unbearable ecstasy. The sound was stolen by Tom's mouth, his tongue miming the action of his fingers inside her as she experienced a release so powerful it left her totally enervated.

The next thing Megan was aware of was Tom lifting her into his arms, her head lolling against his strong shoulder as he carried her into her bedroom. She barely had time to register the fact that he'd fortuitously ended up in her room, which was on the left side of the hall, rather than Sarah's, which was on the right, before she felt his welcome weight on her body.

"Megan, Megan, I knew it would be like this with us. Let me love you, sweetheart. Here, let me help you out of this outfit."

She was naked to his gaze in moments, and it wasn't until then that she realized Tom was still fully dressed. At that same moment she became aware of the phone ringing.

"Let it ring," he said, his eyes reverently appraising her body.

For a moment Megan had no thoughts of answering it. Then she remembered her children weren't safe at home. What if something had happened to Christopher or Sarah? She would never forgive herself. And so, knowing that it was probably Stephanie, or her mother, or one of a dozen other friends, she picked up the phone.

"Hello? He what?" Megan sat up so abruptly that she bumped Tom's chin with her forehead. "Ow! It's nothing. Go on."

Megan was oblivious to Tom's injury, and rubbed her own forehead absently as she listened and talked. "When did it happen? So you took him to the hospital? Where is that? How long ago? Did you call the doctor? What did he say? I'll be right there."

Megan dropped the phone back on the hook and turned on the lamp beside the bed at the same time. The light illuminated *YOU DON'T HAVE TO STAY SINGLE*, which was on her bedside table. She had the presence of mind to turn the book over to hide the title as she climbed off the bed and crossed to her dresser drawers to pull out a pair of jeans and a sweatshirt.

"Do you mind telling me what the hell's going on?" Tom asked, still rubbing his bruised chin.

Megan took one look at him and knew she was dealing with a frustrated, sexually aroused male. "There's been an emergency. I have to go."

Tom was feeling particularly uncharitable at the moment, but what made it worse was his certainty that it was the elusive "other man" in Megan's life that she was rushing off to comfort. "Who got hurt? Who are you leaving this bed to take care of?"

Megan was mortified by Tom's insinuation, but she had a feeling the only explanation that was going to be sufficient right now was the truth—and she shuddered to think how he would react to that. His gaze was hot on hers, watching her as she dressed. It was all very well to touch in the dark, but the lamp was revealing every stretch mark she had. She angled her body away and yanked up her jeans.

"I haven't got time to talk now," she said. "I have to go to the hospital."

"I'll drive."

"There's no need."

"I'll drive."

Knowing he was angry enough to insist, Megan didn't argue. She let him open the right-hand door of his car for her and sat down stiffly inside.

Once he was seated with the engine running he asked, "Where are we going?"

"Jackson Memorial Hospital. Head south on I-95. I'll give you more directions when we get closer." Megan's face was white with fear and her hands were trembling. She clasped them together and closed her eyes, unaware that she'd been murmuring a prayer.

"Who's hurt?" Tom demanded.

"Christopher."

"Who's Christo—"

"My son."

Tom was stunned into silence.

Now that she'd told him that much, Megan couldn't seem to stop talking. Everything came blurting out. "Chris was spending the night with his friend, Jeff. They were playing touch football and Chris tripped and fell. He hit his head on one of the metal water sprinklers in the yard. The doctor thinks he just has a concussion, but they're still doing tests. He hasn't regained consciousness since it happened."

"When was that?"

"Several hours ago."

Tom didn't know what to say. He remembered what he'd been through when his own son had been so ill. But Todd had just been a newborn baby and he and Sally hadn't yet formed the kind of bond that apparently existed between Megan and her son.

"How old is he?"

"He's only eight." The words came out as a moan of anguish.

Tom followed Megan's directions and they soon arrived at the emergency entrance to Jackson Memorial.

"I'll let you out here and go park. I'll join you as soon as—"

Megan didn't wait to hear the rest of what Tom said. She was already on her way inside. She was appalled at what she found. It was easy to ignore the fact that Miami was a big city until you came face to face with the traumatic results of urban life. Knifings, shootings, drug overdoses, wife beatings, heart attacks, car accidents, broken bones—the cacophony of those in pain and those treating their pain was terrifying.

Tom found Megan standing frozen just inside the door and put his arm around her waist, moving her toward the admissions desk.

"We're here to see Christopher Padget," he told the woman in receiving. "Can you tell us where we can find him?"

She typed Christopher's name into a computer and said, "They're running some tests upstairs. You can wait there."

Tom followed the nurse's directions and escorted Megan upstairs to the appropriate nurse's station. As soon as Megan identified herself the nurse said, "It won't be long now. The doctor will be with you as soon as he's finished the tests. You can wait over there."

Christopher's friend, Jeff, and Jeff's mother, Lizabeth Simpson, were sitting in the waiting room.

"I'm so glad you're here," Lizabeth said, rising and rushing forward to hug Megan. "I got worried when I couldn't get you on the phone. It's the waiting that's so terrible. The nurse says we should know something soon."

Jeff was crying and saying it was all his fault, that even though it was getting dark he'd insisted they keep playing. Megan put a hand on his shoulder to comfort him. "I'm sure it was an accident, Jeff. These things happen."

Lizabeth saw the clerical collar Tom wore and said, "A priest, Megan? It's not that serious!"

Megan would have laughed except her sense of humor failed her at the moment. "This is Tom Steele. You remember I told you Tom and I were going to a costume party tonight? He's still wearing his costume."

"Oh, I see," Lizabeth said, only Megan could tell she didn't, really.

"I couldn't reach Sarah to tell her what happened," Lizabeth added. "Do you want to try calling her yourself?"

"Sarah?" Tom asked.

"My daughter." Megan was too worried about Chris to respond to the bemused look on Tom's face other than by saying, "She's spending the night with friends tonight, too."

"How old is Sarah?" His voice was so soft she wouldn't have heard him except that he was speaking into her ear.

"She's fourteen. Almost fifteen."

"Maybe it would be better to wait and call her when you know something definite," Tom suggested.

Megan sighed and wilted onto one of the vinyl-covered couches in the waiting room. "You're right. She'd only worry and there's nothing she can do right now."

Tom sat down beside Megan, wondering why she hadn't said anything to him about her children. Two of them! A boy and a girl—and the girl was four-teen—almost fifteen! But then, he hadn't been forth-right about Todd, either.

Fortunately they didn't have long to wait for news about Chris. The doctor joined them within fifteen minutes of their arrival. "Are you Mrs. Padget?"

Megan jumped up. "Yes, I am."

"And this is Mr. Padget?" he asked, turning and extending his hand to Tom.

"I'm Tom Steele, a friend of the family."

The doctor turned back to Megan. "I must say, Mrs. Padget, that your son is a very lucky little boy."

"Then he's going to be all right?"

"Yes, he is. He regained consciousness half an hour ago. He's got a concussion, and he'll have quite a headache, but our tests didn't show any other prob-lems. He'll have to stay in bed for a while, and then take it easy a little longer, but he should recover fully."

"Thank God," Megan murmured. Without being aware she did so, she leaned back against Tom, whose arms came around to support her. "Can I see him?"

"Certainly."

Tom didn't ask if he could go along, he simply stayed with Megan as the nurse directed her to her son's room. He kept his arm around her as he followed her inside to where a small, towheaded boy lay covered in white sheets except for his head and shoulders.

"Hi, Mom," Chris said in a frail voice.

"Hi, honey. Guess the sprinkler won that one, huh?"

"Yeah. I'm sorry I spoiled your date."

"You didn't spoil anything." Megan felt her face flushing bright red.

"Hi," Chris said, his dark brown eyes locked on Tom. "I'm Chris. Are you going to marry my mom?"

Megan gasped, her face flushing an even brighter red, if that was possible. "Tom and I have only just met—"

"I like your mom a lot," Tom interrupted.

"Yeah. But do you like football?" Chris asked.

A grin slowly widened on Tom's face. "I sure do."

"Good. I'm kinda sleepy, Mom. Will you stay with me?"

"Don't worry, honey. I'll be here."

Megan reassured Lizabeth and Jeff that Chris would be fine and urged them to go home and rest until the next day, when they could visit him. Then she checked with the nurses and found out they were willing to put a folding cot in Chris's room for her.

"It's too late now to call Sarah," Megan said, turning to Tom, "but I don't want her to come home to an empty house tomorrow, either. Would you mind staying at my house—and waiting for her?"

"Won't she be upset to find a stranger there?"

"She knows what you look like."

At Tom's questioning look Megan explained. "She saw you that first day we met, when I was shopping."

"All right. I'll be glad to stay. Do you want me to bring her here?"

"Please. And ask her to bring me some clean things to wear, if you would."

"Sure."

They stood staring awkwardly at one another for a moment before Tom said, "Well, I'd better let you get some rest."

"I'll see you in the morning."

"Right."

Megan watched Tom turn and walk away, wondering what he was thinking. Damn, damn, damn! If only she'd told him the truth when she'd had the chance. When she thought about it she realized he'd taken things quite calmly, considering the fact that she'd lied to him—admittedly by omission—and then left him sexually high and dry. She'd find a way to make it all up to him. Because after tonight there was no hiding from the truth. Tom Steele was a very special man, very possibly the right one for her. And she was going to give them both every chance to find that out for sure.

Seven

————

His Book: "What Do Her Criticisms Mean?"

Are you sure you're feeling up to this, Chris?" Megan asked, brushing a hank of shaggy blond hair back from her son's brow.

"Jeez, Mom, it's been a month. I'm fine."

"He's the same old bonehead," Sarah gibed.

"Sarah, don't talk about your brother that way."

"All I meant was that he's back to normal."

Megan rolled her eyes at Sarah's not-too-subtle insult.

"I'm really looking forward to this football game, too," Sarah said.

"Is it the game you're looking forward to? Or spending more time with Tom?" Megan questioned.

"Both. He's a really nice guy, Mom. And he knows a lot about a lot of things."

"Yeah," Chris agreed. "And he sure can throw a football better than you, Mom."

Megan acknowledged the spurt of irritation she experienced at her children's open admiration of Tom Steele, and immediately felt petty and foolish. After all, it was a blessing that Tom had found a way to explain the new math concepts to Sarah that hadn't left her confused. And Chris had basked in the approval that only a man could give to a little boy who was seeking a role model. But she could see it was going to be harder to share her children with Tom than she'd thought. She'd become possessive of their attentions over the past five years when they'd only had a mother to turn to.

When Tom had shown up with Sarah at the hospital on the morning after Chris's accident, Megan had discovered that he wasn't annoyed by the fact that she had two children; he was positively overjoyed.

"I love kids," he'd explained when they'd had time alone to talk. "I'd have had a houseful of them if it had been up to me. Have you thought about having any more?"

"Not lately," Megan had answered evasively. "Besides, I'm getting a little old to be having babies."

"Really? You don't look old." He'd reached up and playfully traced the small wrinkles around her eyes with his thumbs.

"Character lines," they'd said almost in unison.

They'd laughed, and she'd felt warm inside with the sound of Tom's rich, booming laughter. But she hadn't admitted to him that her age had nothing to do with the fact that she wouldn't be having any more children.

"How old are you?" she'd asked. "I see a strand or two of gray in here." She'd run her fingers through his hair, marveling at its soft texture.

"I'll be thirty-six next August," he'd replied with a relaxed smile. "Is that old enough for you?"

I'm four years older than you are! "My birthday's in August, too," she'd volunteered. "Isn't that a co-incidence?" but she didn't volunteer her age. And she noticed he didn't ask.

She'd thought a lot in the past month about whether it was fair to deceive Tom the way she had—to suggest that she had a choice about whether or not to have any more babies. He apparently wanted more children—a son in his image, he'd said. She could tell by the way he acted with Sarah and Chris that he'd make a wonderful father. In fact that was the source of a great deal of her current aggravation. Her children seemed to forget she existed whenever Tom was around.

She was still feeling annoyed when the source of her irritation arrived at the door.

"Hi, Tom!" Chris shouted, racing to let him in.

"Hello, Tom!" Sarah followed her younger brother to the door with equal excitement.

Megan watched as Tom stepped inside, lifted Chris clear off the ground and gave him a quick hug before settling the boy in the crook of one arm. Chris's arms looped easily around Tom's neck. Meanwhile, Tom slipped his other arm around Sarah's waist and pulled her snugly to his side. Megan noticed how Sarah's whole body leaned into Tom, evidencing her trust in him. In little more than an instant three persons had joined ranks...and become connected. She knew it was ridiculous, but she felt excluded.

"So how are the two of you today?" Tom's cheeks dimpled as he grinned. "Ready to watch the Dolphins dump the Colts?"

"You bet!" Chris replied.

Megan saw the pleasure in her children's faces mirrored in Tom's gaze as he looked back at them. Then he lifted his eyes and met hers. She knew the distress he was seeing on her face confused him, and she quickly turned away to get her feelings under control. The next thing she knew Tom's arms were around her waist and she felt his broad, muscular chest against her back. He was strong and capable...capable of taking control of her children and her life.

"Hello, Megan," he whispered in her ear. "I missed you."

Megan blushed, since it had only been a matter of a few hours since she'd sent him out the front door. They'd spent the better part of the previous night and early-morning hours necking on her living-room couch.

"Tom...the children—"

"Have a pretty good idea how I feel about you," he said, nuzzling her neck and sending involuntary shivers down her spine.

Megan was feeling crotchety and contrary. She pulled away from him and said, her voice sharp, "You've made sure of that, haven't you?"

When Megan turned to face Tom she saw the shock and hurt in his eyes. What was wrong with her? She hadn't meant to say such a mean thing. But instead of the apology she knew she should make she said, "We're going to be late if we don't leave right now. Sarah, Chris, go on out to the car. We'll be with you in a minute."

Megan's throat closed in pain as she met the accusing looks on her children's faces before they turned to leave.

"I'll get the cooler," Tom said.

"I can carry it," Megan countered.

"But why should you have to when I'm here?"

Megan watched the muscles in Tom's arms bulge beneath his short-sleeved cotton knit shirt as he lifted the cooler. She watched a frown form when he realized how heavy it was. "What's in this thing?"

"I packed some extra sodas."

"For us and what army?" he said, laughing.

"It's a warm day. I thought we might get thirsty," Megan replied, more than a hint of asperity in her voice.

"It's all right, Megan. I think I can handle the extra weight."

But Megan refused to be soothed by his attempt at conciliation. "Give it to me." She stepped in front of Tom and reached for the handholds.

Tom stopped and looked down at her as though she'd lost her mind. "What the hell's going on, Megan? You've done nothing but snipe at me since I walked in the door. Is it that time of the month?"

"How dare you make such a remark!"

"Give me another explanation for the way you're behaving," he challenged.

"I don't have to explain anything to you."

"Maybe not. But I'm not moving another step until you do."

"Maybe I don't like the way you take over and do things before you're asked!" she retorted.

His voice was so soft she had to listen hard to hear his reply. "Is that what you really think? That I'm trying to take over?"

"Aren't you?"

Tom set the cooler down on the dining-room table and grasped Megan by the arms. "Let's get something straight right now. I care a great deal about you, Megan. And I think the world of Sarah and Chris. But the last thing I want to do is *impose* myself on this family. Any time you want me out of here all you have to do is say the word. Is that understood?"

Megan stared at the tuft of hair that showed at the opening of Tom's shirt, too ashamed to look him in the eye. But he wasn't about to let her get away with that kind of cowardice. His forefinger levered its way under her chin and tilted her face upward. Still she kept her gaze down, seeing only his tightly compressed lips and jutting chin through her lowered lashes.

"All right, Megan. What's it to be?"

She cleared her throat. "I may have exaggerated the situation . . . a bit."

"And?"

"And I hope you'll spend the day with us even though I've been acting like a total idiot."

Tom chuckled. "*Is* it that time of the month?"

Megan snorted and jerked her chin away from his touch. "For heaven's sake! So what if it is? What does that have to do with anything?"

Tom's chuckle became a full-throated laugh. "Nothing. Let's get out of here. I promised the kids we could throw a football around the parking lot before the game."

Megan watched as Tom hefted the cooler again and headed out the door ahead of her. Why couldn't she have been more honest with Tom about her fears? Why couldn't she have admitted that it was going to take her some time to adjust to the children's growing reliance on him? Why couldn't she have just said that she was crazy in love with him and it scared her to death to think he might not be just as much in love with her?

Tom spent the first half of the game watching Megan carefully when she wasn't looking. What he saw confused and worried him. She was enjoying the contest on the field, all right. But her eyes lacked sparkle, and the lilt was missing from her laugh. And he couldn't think of a single reason that should be so. They'd spent some part of every day together for the past month since Chris's accident. He hadn't pressed her to make love simply because they hadn't had the privacy they both desired. However, they'd pleasured one another in different ways. He didn't doubt her attraction to him, nor his to her. So what was wrong?

At that moment one of the several men who'd been drinking beer at the far end of the aisle stood up and carelessly began making his way toward the stadium stairs. In the process he stepped on toes and spilled beer on those he passed. Tom was watching him in disgust when the man stepped on Megan's toe. As she yelped and jerked her foot out of his way he lost his balance and spilled part of his tall cup of beer on Sarah. He turned on Megan snarling, "Sonofa—"

The man never got a chance to finish. Tom wasn't even aware of moving. He simply found himself with two handfuls of the man's shirt in his fists. He lifted the drunken man off the ground and rasped in a deadly voice, "Apologize to both of them. Now."

"'Scuse me," the man slurred, his eyes wide with fright, both hands scrunching the top of his paper cup.

"Now I suggest you find somewhere else to watch the rest of the game."

Tom lifted the drunk and set him down beyond Chris, watching with steely eyes until he was gone. Then he sat down with a calm that was dangerous for its quiet. "Are you both all right?"

"I'm a little wet," Sarah said, her nose wrinkled with distaste as she brushed off her shorts. "But I'll dry."

"And you, Megan?"

"I could have taken care of the situation if you'd given me the chance. He was drunk. Do you really think it was necessary to manhandle him like that?"

"Nobody hurts my fam—" Tom bit his tongue to catch himself. But from the look in Megan's eyes he was too late.

"We're missing the game." She abruptly turned away from him to stare at the field.

Megan hadn't mentioned the incident again, but she'd been distant, silent. And when he'd tried to kiss her good night, she'd stiffened. He was hurt, but afraid to ask her what was wrong, afraid she didn't care for him as much as he cared for her.

That evening, after he'd dropped Megan and her kids off, he didn't go straight home. The house he'd rented was too empty, and he was too frustrated by the day's events. He'd proved to himself that with the right motivation, he could be violent. He found himself heading for Randy and Irene's place.

"Well, well. Look what the cat dragged in, Irene."

"Tom! What a nice surprise. You look like you got a little sun today. Did you go to the game?"

"Yeah."

"But not alone," Randy surmised.

"Naw."

"Megan Padget?"

"Yeah."

"I've seen happier faces on cadavers," Randy said. "Pull up a chair and tell big brother all about it."

"Would a beer help?" Irene asked.

Tom grimaced. "Yeah."

Randy turned to his wife and said, "Loquacious, isn't he?" He sat down in a comfortable chair across from the couch where Tom had sprawled. "The only words in your vocabulary tonight seem to be *yeah* and *naw*. Want to talk about what's wrong?"

"Yeah."

"Did she throw you out?"

"Naw."

"Well, that's something at least."

Irene handed Tom an ice-cold bottle of beer. "Would a woman's perspective help?"

Tom took several swallows of the drink. "Yeah."

Irene sat on the arm of Randy's chair and leaned back. "So, what do you want to know?"

"Why would Megan suddenly start to criticize everything I do?"

"Give me an example," Irene said.

Tom thought of the incident with the drunk, but realized it was too revealing of his own feelings. There were enough other examples that would serve his purpose. "Today when we were at the game, I offered to buy Sarah some peanuts. Megan said that was a dumb idea, because it would just make a mess. Later, Chris spilled his drink and I said I'd buy him another one. Megan said since Chris had spilled it he could get his own soda."

"Both incidents occurred when you made suggestions to her children," Irene noted.

"I guess they did. So what?"

"You haven't read all of *HOW TO MARRY THE WOMAN OF YOUR DREAMS*, have you?" Randy asked.

"Why do you say that?"

"Because there's a whole chapter entitled, 'What Her Criticisms Mean.'"

"I assume you've read it," Tom said. "So why don't you condense it for me?"

Randy quoted:

A woman doesn't criticize a man without reason. Unfortunately, what she says and what she really means aren't always the same thing.

"Would you mind translating that into English?" Tom said irritably.

Irene leaned forward and put a hand on Tom's shoulder. "It means that something could be bothering Megan about your relationship with her children."

"But I love her kids!"

"More than you love Megan?" Irene asked.

"Of course not!"

"Have you told Megan that?"

"I would have if I'd thought it was necessary. She knows how I feel about her."

"Are you sure?"

Tom was silent for a moment. "It couldn't be anything as simple as that."

Irene shrugged. "I'm not saying it is. But it might be. How long has Megan had the children to herself?"

"She was divorced five years ago. Her ex-husband died two years ago."

"She's had a lot of time to establish a close relationship with her children. Maybe you're threatening that relationship."

"I don't want to take away from Megan's closeness to the kids. I only want to be a part of..." Tom remembered Megan's reaction to his slip in referring to her and her children as his family. "She doesn't want me to be a part of their family?" Tom's brow furrowed in thought. "Do you think that's it?"

"Only Megan knows for sure, Tom. My suggestion is that you talk to her," Randy said. "And read that chapter on a woman's criticisms. Maybe it'll give you some ideas about how to handle the situation."

"I guess it's worth a try anyway." Tom leaned forward to finish his beer. "I'd better get home. It's late."

Randy and Irene both rose to see Tom to the door.

"If you feel like talking some more, you know where we are," Randy said.

"Thanks." Tom gently cuffed Randy on the chin with his fist. "It's a comfort to know that. I mean it."

When Tom got home, he pulled his birthday book from under a pile of papers that had accumulated on top of it and turned to the chapter entitled, "What Her Criticisms Mean."

Don't ignore what a woman says in pique or anger. Often that is when she's being most honest.

In a day and age where communication between the sexes is clouded with confusion, you can't afford to bury your head in the sand and refuse to hear words that may hurt.

Was that what he'd done? Refused to hear what he didn't find to his liking? What had Megan said when he'd picked up the cooler this morning? Something about taking control of things when he hadn't been asked. What *exactly* had she said? Tom thought for a moment and heard Megan speaking again.

Maybe I don't like the way you take over and do things before you're asked.

Take over. Take control. He couldn't be making the same mistakes now that he'd made so long ago with Sally. He no longer needed to be the one in charge. He'd learned from his past mistakes. He'd changed. Or so he'd thought. What had Megan said after the incident with the drunk?

I could have handled the situation if you'd given me the chance.

It was hard to accept the fact that Megan didn't want his help. Not with lifting and carrying. Not with her children. Not even with handling a drunk. What *did* she want from him?

He turned back to his book, looking for more answers.

When in doubt as to what a woman is thinking, ask her.

It wasn't that simple, Tom thought. He'd already asked Megan a couple of times today what was wrong and she hadn't given him a straight answer. He read the next few lines with a grim look on his face.

If you can't get her to tell you what she's thinking, tell her what you're thinking and see if you're both on the same wavelength.

Tom picked up the phone and dialed Megan's number, even though it was late and even though he knew she was probably already in bed. He felt an undeniable sense of urgency. This couldn't wait. He had to repair whatever damage he'd caused today, and he wanted to do it now.

"Who's calling?"

It wasn't until Tom heard Megan's voice, husky with sleep, that he actually looked at the clock and saw it was long past midnight. Hell, maybe her defenses were down and he'd get the answers he sought.

"I couldn't sleep," he said.

"I'll let you come over and make breakfast tomorrow at six a.m. Then maybe you'll get tired at a decent hour," she mumbled.

"I've been thinking, Megan."

"That's nice."

"Are you awake?"

"I guess so."

"I've been thinking...."

"Hmm?"

"Maybe I've been sticking my nose in where it doesn't belong with regard to Sarah and Chris, interfering in things that were better left alone."

Tom waited, but Megan didn't say anything. At last he heard, "Hmm."

Tom's chest hurt. She wasn't contradicting him. He forced himself to go on. "So maybe it would be better if I stayed away from you and the kids for a while."

Silence again.

Tom's stomach felt queasy. "Did you hear what I said?"

"Hmm."

"Am I right?"

"You know best, Tom."

Tom's head felt as if burly blacksmiths with heavy hammers were pounding away inside. "I won't be seeing you for a while then."

"If you say so."

"Good night, Megan."

"Good night, Tom."

"I love you," he whispered.

"Hmm."

Tom hung up the phone in a state of shock. He looked down at the book in his lap.

Be willing to accept the answers you get, even if they weren't the ones you expected. Not every woman is right for every man.

Tom grabbed the book and threw it across the room with all his might. It slammed against the wall with a resounding *thwack* and fell in a ruffled heap on the hardwood floor.

Eight

Her Book: "Meeting His Mother"

The next morning Megan could vaguely recollect getting a phone call from Tom the night before, but couldn't remember much of the conversation. She'd been so keyed up after the day they'd spent together that she'd taken a sleeping pill to help her get some rest. She'd only wakened long enough to answer the phone and then put it back on the hook when she heard the irritating bleep that told her Tom had long since hung up at the other end.

She'd tried calling him all day, but his answering machine was on. She caught up with Stephanie at lunch and asked, "Have you seen Tom around on campus today?"

"Haven't you heard? He's gone to Panama."

"Panama?"

"Seems the U.S. ambassador needed some advice."

Megan stared at the gently swaying fronds of the palm trees lining the campus quadrangle and tried to think calm thoughts. "He didn't even call me to say he was going."

Or was that what he'd called to say last night? Megan just couldn't remember.

"When is he supposed to be back?" she asked Stephanie.

"Why are you asking me these questions? He's your boyfriend."

Megan glared at Stephanie who quickly said, "I heard from the dean's secretary that he's only supposed to be gone for a couple of days."

But a couple of days turned into two weeks. In fact, Tom still hadn't contacted Megan by the time Thanksgiving vacation arrived. As much as she'd objected to Tom involving himself in her children's lives, his absence was deeply felt at a table set for three.

"This is a time for thanksgiving. Why the long faces?" she demanded as she served up plates heaped with honey-glazed ham, twice-baked sweet potatoes, asparagus, blueberry muffins and warm port-wine-and-cranberry sauce.

"I wish Tom were here," Chris said.

Sarah mashed her fork into her sweet potatoes, making designs. "I miss him. Mom, do you think there's a chance that you and he...I mean, he really seemed to like you. Why hasn't he come to see us?"

"I told you he went to Panama," Megan answered.

"But he didn't even call to say goodbye," Chris said. "I thought he liked me."

"He does like you," Megan reassured her son.

"Then why hasn't he called?"

"I suspect because he's been very busy. He's doing an important job. He probably doesn't have—" Megan cut herself off as she realized what she'd been about to say—that he hadn't had time. Surely Tom could have found a few moments in the past two weeks to call and let them know he was thinking of them. If he was.

If only she could remember that telephone call!

As they were eating their pumpkin pie the phone rang.

"I'll get it," Chris shouted as he jumped up from the table. "I'll bet it's Tom."

But it wasn't Tom. It was Irene Steele.

"Tom called Randy to say he'll be back on Monday. He was invited to spend Thanksgiving with the ambassador's family and decided to stay. Anyway, what I wanted to ask was whether you and your children could come to a barbecue Randy and I are giving next Saturday. Please say yes."

Megan's brain was still trying to cope with the fact that Tom had found time to call his brother but not her and her children. It was hard not to take out her growing anger with Tom on Irene. If the fact that Tom had ignored them meant he planned to do a replay of his former disappearing act, this invitation from Irene might be the only chance she'd have to confront him about his insensitivity to her children's feelings—not to mention her own.

"We'd love to come," she heard herself say. "What time do you want us there?"

Megan had expected to have trouble finding the street where Irene and Randy Steele lived because Coral Gables was a maze of banyon-shaded boulevards that curved and wound without any rhyme or reason. The task was living up to her worst expectations. To add to her worries, Chris was bouncing around in the car like a parakeet gone wild in a glass cage. Megan knew he was just excited—and a little worried—about seeing Tom again. That explained his behavior, but it didn't make it any less nerve-racking.

Chris threw his upper body halfway over the front seat to complain loudly about his sister. "Mom, Sarah pinched me."

"Only after he pulled my hair!"

"Sit down, Chris! If I have to stop suddenly you'll go right through the windshield."

"When are we going to get there, Mom? I'm hungry," he complained.

"I don't see how you could be. You had two granola bars and a container of yogurt before we left home."

"That was over an hour ago," Sarah pointed out. She leaned over the seat beside Chris. "Where are we, Mom? Are we lost?"

Megan looked down at the directions Irene had given her over the phone, then back up again, searching for the concrete corner stones used for street signs in Coral Gables. "I'm sure it's not far now, Sarah. If

you'll both sit down and sit still for a few more minutes, we'll be there.''

But it was half an hour later that Megan finally
backtracked and found the large Spanish-style house
she was looking for.

Megan gave Irene a quick hug before turning to
shake Randy's hand. Randy had about the same build
as Tom, but he was slightly shorter, and his features
weren't nearly as distinctive. It was like comparing a
cougar and a leopard. They were both dangerous cats,
but the beauty of the leopard took your breath away.

"Where's Tom?" Chris asked as soon as he realized the man he'd come to see wasn't there.

"He should be here soon," Irene answered. "How
would you like to play in the backyard with Charlie
until he arrives?"

"Who's Charlie?"

"Come and see," Irene said mysteriously as she led
Chris out the back door.

Sarah's curiosity got the better of her. "I think I'll
go, too."

Megan was left alone with Randy.

"Charlie is our Afghan hound," he explained. "She
just had a litter of six pups."

"Sarah and Chris will love seeing them." Megan
wasn't sure what to say next, because the obvious topic
of discussion was Tom—who hadn't called her once
the entire week he'd been back. Nor had she picked up
the phone. She'd waited until today to talk with him,
knowing that what she had to discuss was better said
face-to-face.

"I'm glad we have a chance to talk before Tom gets here," Randy said.

Megan had been so totally lost in her thoughts that she hadn't realized Randy had closed the distance between them. He was now standing directly across from her, his feet planted far apart, his white-knuckled hands in fists on his hips. She recognized again the threat of danger she'd felt upon meeting him. She could see he was angry, but she had no idea why. He didn't leave her in suspense for long.

"I want to know why you let my brother fall in love with you and your kids if you weren't serious about a permanent relationship with him."

"Not serious? He's the one who stopped seeing me!"

"That's not what I heard."

"Then you heard wrong. The last time I saw or spoke with Tom was three weeks ago. My children were devastated when he left for Panama without a word, and he hasn't contacted any of us since. You tell me how your brother could let two impressionable children fall in love with him and then turn his back on them!"

"Why don't you ask me yourself."

Megan whirled to find Tom standing in the doorway. She felt a fierce rush of pleasure at seeing him and quickly tamped it down. This was a golden opportunity to confront Tom about her grievances and she didn't intend to let it pass her by. "Do you deny that you left for Panama without a word to me or the children?"

"No."

"Do you deny that you haven't bothered to pick up the phone and call for three weeks?"

"No."

"Do you deny that you've been avoiding me for the past week since you've been back?"

"No."

Megan turned back to confront Randy, her hands on her hips. "Do you still think I'm responsible for ending my relationship with your brother?"

"Wait a minute," Tom said, putting his hand on Megan's shoulder and turning her back around to face him. "Do you deny that you told me—on several occasions—during the last day we spent together that I was sticking my nose in where it didn't belong?"

Megan flushed. "I may have—"

"Do you deny that when I suggested it might be better if I stayed away from you and the kids for a while that you agreed it would be for the best?"

"What? I most certainly do deny it! Whatever gave you such an idea?"

"You did," Tom said between gritted teeth.

"When? I never said any such thing."

"You're conveniently forgetting my phone call the night before I left for Panama. I know what I heard, Megan."

There was a moment of charged silence while Megan assimilated the fact that she must have said something to Tom while she'd been half asleep. "I know you called . . . that is I remember answering the phone and hanging it up again. But Tom, I don't remember anything else you said that night. And I certainly don't remember asking you to stay away! I'd taken a sleeping pill and—"

Tom nearly crushed Megan as his arms folded around her. "God, all the time we've wasted because of a stupid misunderstanding!"

Megan gripped him tightly around the waist as she hid her face in the curve of his shoulder, breathing deeply of his male scent. She stood on tiptoe to press her cheek against his throat. "Oh, Tom, I would never, never suggest you stay away. Don't you know I need you? Sarah and Chris need you."

His mouth slanted onto hers, his tongue probing. She willingly opened to him, her arms sliding up and around his neck, her fingertips tunneling into the shaggy hair at his nape. It was several minutes before they came up for air.

"The children—"

Tom looked up long enough to see that Randy was gone. "My brother'll keep them in the backyard for a while longer. Oh, Megan, I've been slowly dying the past three weeks without you. I missed you. I missed the kids. What have you all been doing?"

"I think first I'd like an explanation for how you could think I didn't want to see you anymore."

Tom wasn't about to explain to Megan that he'd been following the advice in a book designed to help him find a wife. It was too humiliating. "I guess I got my wires crossed. You made it pretty clear you could do things by yourself, that you didn't need my help."

Megan took Tom's hand and pulled him over to the couch so they could sit down together. "I've been on my own a long time, Tom. It's hard to share the kids, and myself, with you. But I'm trying—"

Tom cut her off with a quick, hard kiss. "I promise not to go off half-cocked next time. Now, if we don't catch up with the rest of the gang I'm going to end up hauling you off to one of Randy's bedrooms."

Megan automatically linked her arm around Tom's waist as they rose and headed outside together.

Sarah's and Chris's welcome was so enthusiastic Tom was literally bowled over onto the grass. Tears burned at the back of Megan's eyes as she watched Tom hug her daughter and tickle her son until all three were laughing so hard they were gasping for air.

Irene walked over to stand beside Megan and watch her brother-in-law's antics. "He'll make a wonderful father for those two kids. It's a shame Sally doesn't let him spend more time with Todd. He's about the same age as Chris if I recall correctly."

"Todd?"

Irene's eyes widened in alarm and her hand came up to cover her mouth. "I've stuck my foot in it, haven't I? Tom hasn't told you about his son?"

Megan shook her head no.

Irene put a hand on the arms Megan had crossed protectively in front of her. "Ask him. He'll tell you what you want to know."

Megan kept telling herself all afternoon that it wasn't such a bad thing that Tom hadn't mentioned Todd. After all, she was keeping an equally important secret from him, so what right did she have to be hurt? She cried inside because she'd wanted to be the one to give him that son and couldn't. It was too late for that. Much, much too late.

It wasn't until Sarah and Chris were in bed later that evening that Megan finally asked Tom about Todd. They were lying on the couch together, their bodies aligned with one another.

Tom's hands cupped Megan's breast possessively, and he dipped his head down to kiss the pulse at her throat. "God, I've missed you," he said with a groan.

Megan felt a frisson of desire skitter down her spine and knew that if she didn't speak now, in a few moments neither of them would be doing any talking.

"Is it true that you have a son?"

Tom slowly sat up, rearranging Megan sideways in his lap with his arm supporting her back. He turned her so he could see her face. "How did you find out?"

"Irene. Why didn't you tell me yourself?"

"I try not to think about Todd too much. He was very sick as a child and spent a lot of time in the hospital. I hardly had a chance to get to know him before Sally and I divorced. Sally took him and moved all the way to California, so I can't be with him as often as I'd like. I've only seen him a few times—for a couple of weeks total, maybe—since he was born."

"How old is he?"

"Eight."

Megan looked up into Tom's eyes. "Is that why you spend so much time with Chris? Because he's a substitute for your own son?"

Megan saw the pain in Tom's expression and knew she'd misjudged him. "I'm sorry." She ran a hand through her hair in agitation. "You said you wanted children. I thought it was because you didn't have any of your own.''

"I would like more children." His voice was soft, dreamy almost. "I'd like to make Sarah and Chris mine.''

"Oh, Tom, I—" Megan's voice broke in a sob of mixed pain and pleasure as she leaned against the hard wall of Tom's chest. How could she marry him without telling him the truth? But would he want her when he knew she couldn't give him any more children?

"I'm hoping now that Todd is a little older Sally will let him visit me in the summer. Do you think Todd and Chris will get along?''

"They'll probably fight like cats and dogs, but that's normal.''

"Megan, there's something else I wanted to ask before... before we had our misunderstanding." He tipped Megan's chin up so he could see her eyes. "I'd like for you and the kids to meet my mother and stepfather.''

Megan felt her face flushing. She couldn't help remembering what *YOU DON'T HAVE TO STAY SINGLE* had to say about this all-important step.

When a man introduces you to his family it means he's thinking about marriage.

"When would we meet them?" she asked. "Didn't you say your mother lives in San Antonio?''

"I'd like to fly you and the kids out there with me over Christmas.''

"Oh, Tom, we can't.''

Megan had been watching his face so she saw the disappointment flash in his eyes before he was able to hide it.

"It's not that I don't want to," Megan explained. "It's just that it's so close to Christmas and I've already made plans with Gary's parents—the children's grandparents—to come here for Christmas. Then Sarah and Chris are going to spend New Year's with my folks. I'm sorry."

Megan was as disappointed as Tom was. "I wish there were some way—"

"What about leaving Sarah and Chris with your parents and joining me in San Antonio by yourself?"

"I couldn't do that!"

"Why not?"

"I haven't left the kids alone with anyone for any length of time for—"

"For too long, I'm sure," Tom interrupted. "Come to San Antonio for New Year's," he coaxed. "I want my mother to meet you."

And what if she didn't go? Would it make a difference to their relationship? Megan thought not, but she wanted to please Tom . . . and she relished the thought of some time alone with him.

"All right, I'll come."

Tom flashed a wicked grin. "I missed Thanksgiving without you. Shall we celebrate now?"

Megan settled back in his arms and traced the line of his jaw with her forefinger. She left her thumb test the fullness of his mouth, then lifted her head up to nip at his lower lip and worry it gently with her teeth. Before he could catch her mouth with his she drew back teasingly. Her hands cupped his face and she could feel the roughness of the day's growth of beard under her fingertips. She brought his face down to hers and kissed his cheeks, his eyelids, his nose and his chin. Finally she reached for his mouth.

At that point, Tom's patience gave up the ghost. His lips descended, capturing Megan's with a fire that caused her blood to race. His hands sought out the pleasure points on her body, touching with need, with hope, with love. Their clothes were a barrier, and soon buttons had been undone and cloth shoved out of the way so that flesh met willing flesh.

The sound of Chris's voice jarred them both. Tom sat up abruptly, nearly dumping Megan on the floor. She grasped his arm to help her stand, and began frantically rebuttoning her blouse and pulling up her shorts as Tom zipped up his jeans and rearranged his disheveled shirt.

"I'm coming, darling. I'll be right there," Megan shouted. Thank goodness Chris hadn't come looking for her.

"Is Tom still here?" Chris called from the bedroom.

Tom cleared his throat, in an effort to rid his voice of the last vestiges of passion. "I'm here, Chris."

"Will you come in and talk to me?"

Tom looked to Megan for concurrence, and when he got it said, "I'll be right there."

Megan followed after Tom, helping him tuck his shirt back into his jeans.

Tom sat down on the bed beside Chris. "What did you want to talk about, Tiger?"

"You're not going to go away and leave us again, are you?"

"I'll be going to see my mom and stepfather for Christmas, but I won't go without saying goodbye, and you'll know when I'm coming back."

"Will you give me a hug good-night?"

Megan watched as the two men in her life exchanged a masculine embrace.

"Good night, Tiger."

"Good night, Tom."

Megan took her turn hugging Chris and tucked him in snugly before she left the room with Tom.

Once they were back in the living room Tom said, "I'd better go." His mouth came down hard, his tongue searching, but he forced himself to pull back. "I'm looking forward to having some time alone with you in San Antonio."

"Me, too."

Megan could still taste him on her lips after he'd left. She ached. It was terrible to feel like this. But it was wonderful to know that soon she'd be able to slake her hunger for Tom.

That night she lay in bed with a silly grin on her face. her world was right again. She felt a bit of trepidation about meeting Tom's mother and consoled herself by picking up *YOU DON'T HAVE TO STAY SINGLE* and turning to the chapter called, "Meeting His Mother."

Certain rules of etiquette and decorum apply when you meet a man's mother for the first time. Expect her values to be different and be ready to adjust accordingly. Follow her lead.

One last warning: Watch your step! Your relationship with his mother is laced with pitfalls.

Megan fell asleep imagining herself curtsying to a plump little woman dressed in a pillbox hat, conservative suit, white gloves and pumps.

Three weeks later Megan was sitting at the San Antonio airport waiting for Tom to arrive, wearing an outfit designed to make her look as sexless as possible. She knew it was ridiculous, but the more she'd read, the more she'd been sure it was important to dress, act and speak conservatively around Tom's mother.

Tom had missed Megan more than he'd thought possible, and he was impatient to hold her in his arms, to catch the sweet gardenia scent of her hair as he tasted her mouth with his. When he finally spied her he realized why he hadn't noticed her sooner. She was wearing a shapeless gray-green dress that made her fade into the airport wall. Her face was pale and drawn, and she didn't seem to be wearing any makeup. Her beautiful golden-brown hair was pulled back severely and hidden in a knot behind her head. He wasn't conscious of the frown on his face as he approached her.

Megan caught sight of Tom just before he reached her. He didn't look the least bit pleased to see her. Had he changed his mind about her in the three weeks they'd been separated?

"Megan? Is something wrong? Are the kids okay?"

"No, everyone's fine. What makes you ask?" He didn't even take her in his arms, and she felt too uncertain to walk forward the few steps necessary to put herself there. This wasn't the romantic reunion she'd imagined, where she flew into Tom's arms and he slanted his lips onto hers.

Tom shook his head, still frowning at her. "I just thought..." He couldn't tell her she looked like death warmed over. But he wasn't about to lie and say she looked great, either. He settled for the one thing he could say with complete honesty. "I'm glad you're here."

Then he stepped forward and folded her into his arms—and everything was wonderful.

"I missed you." He groaned with pleasure as his lips came down to devour hers.

Megan was still reeling from the potent kiss when Tom began hurrying her toward the baggage-claim area.

"I promised Mom we'd be back in time for supper. Your plane was late so we'll have to hurry to make it."

They were in the car and headed away from the airport before Megan worked up the courage to say, "What's your mother like?"

Tom grinned. "It's a little late to be asking that, isn't it? You'll be seeing for yourself in a few minutes."

Megan smiled bleakly. "I suppose you're right. Is there anything I should know before I meet her?"

"Like what?"

She shrugged. "I don't know. I guess I thought...if there was a subject I shouldn't talk about or anything."

"Just be yourself, Megan, and she'll love you."

Megan's heart was pounding with fear when she stepped inside the foyer of the huge old two-story Victorian home in Alamo Heights.

They were greeted by a small, perfectly coifed woman wearing three-inch heels and an elegant hot-pink silk pantsuit with a deep décolletage. There was a welcoming smile on her face and a twinkle in her deep-set blue eyes.

No pillbox hat, no white gloves, no pumps. Megan wondered what other false preconceptions she harbored about this woman. *How I wish I'd worn something with buttons down the front for Tom!*

"I'm so glad you were able to get here in time," Tom's mother said in a rumbling contralto. "You know how the General is, Tom. Cocktails at 7:30, dinner promptly at 8:00, come hail or high water. I'm so glad to meet you, my dear. Tom has told me so much about you and your two wonderful children. I hope you had a good Christmas. We had a perfectly marvelous one here, except I do miss the snow. Tom, take Megan's suitcase to the downstairs bedroom while I get her something to drink before dinner. What can I get you, dear?"

Megan found herself bereft of Tom, ensconced in a cushioned wicker settee on a glassed-in porch, holding an icy margarita in her hand, and wondering why she had been so worried about meeting this perfectly charming woman.

"Please call me Isabel," Tom's mother said. She slipped off her high heels and tucked her bare toes under her on the couch. "I was surprised when Tom asked if he could invite a woman to come visit. I thought he'd decided never to marry again."

Megan choked on a sip of margarita. "Uh. Tom and I haven't spoken about marriage."

She felt Isabel's intense gaze examining her. She decided to follow Isabel's lead, and slipped off her shoes, tucking her legs under her. Then she self-consciously straightened the ugly gray-green dress, which had bunched around her waist.

"Are you pregnant, my dear?"

Megan sat up with a start, her eyes wide, and managed to spill a good portion of her margarita on her lap. "Of course not!"

Without batting an eyelash, Isabel began dabbing Megan's dress with a handful of napkins from the coffee table. "I apologize for my frankness. It's just that your dress has so very much extra material in it that I thought...oh, well, in due time. I did so hope for more grandchildren."

Megan heard the wistful tone in Isabel's voice and could have cried. Would Tom's mother be so pleasant if she knew Megan's marriage to Tom would deprive her of any more grandchildren?

"I must say you're not exactly what I expected from Tom's description of you," Isabel said, filling the silence.

"Oh?"

"I thought you'd be taller. And Tom said your hair was honey brown, but I think it's more golden. Yes, definitely golden. But he was right about your eyes. They are the most marvelous color."

Megan felt herself turning red.

"What has Mother said to have you blushing already?" Tom asked as he entered the room.

Isabel turned her cheek for Tom's kiss. "I've been telling her how lovely she is. And that I expect you'll be proposing soon."

Megan saw Tom's scowl and cringed inwardly. So, Isabel was wrong and he wasn't thinking about marriage. Megan watched as he forcibly rearranged his features into a neutral expression. Then he crossed and sat down beside her on the settee, so close that she could feel the heat of him down her entire side.

He casually slipped an arm around her. "Enjoying your drink?" Then, without any warning, his lips dropped to nuzzle her neck.

Megan struggled to keep from spilling what little margarita was left in the glass. "Uh...my drink is fine. Salty." She sat up abruptly, moving away from Tom's nuzzling mouth, and grabbed several napkins from the coffee table to keep her hands busy. She felt a prickling sensation and looked up, meeting Isabel's perceptive gaze.

She knows I'm in love with her son.

Nine

Her Book: "Getting Him to Pop the Question"
His Book: "Avoiding Cold Feet When It's Time to
Commit"

Once Isabel had voiced the possibility of Megan
marrying Tom, Megan couldn't get it off her mind.
She'd avoided Tom's eyes the rest of the evening, sure
that if she looked at him he'd guess what she was
thinking. She was remembering what she'd read in
YOU DON'T HAVE TO STAY SINGLE about how to
get a man to propose.

*Go places where people will treat you as though
you're already a married couple; go shopping for
the kind of items that will furnish a home; talk to*

him in terms of the future; and last, but not least,
let him know you love him and want to spend the
rest of your life with him.

His mother was doing a fine job of treating them as
though they were already married, and between them
they surely had enough furniture for two houses. That
left only speaking to Tom of the future and admitting
that she loved him. But before she could do that she
had a confession to make.

After supper that evening, Isabel and the General,
whom Megan had found not at all stiff and general-
like, both excused themselves and headed upstairs to
bed, leaving Megan and Tom alone on the couch in
front of the cheery fireplace in the living room.

Megan smiled at Tom and he smiled back. Suddenly she was afraid of what he'd say when she con-
fessed the secret she'd kept from him. Couldn't the
truth wait a little bit longer? Couldn't she hold on to
what she had and forget about the future? She leaned
her head against his shoulder and felt his arm encircle
her warmly. It felt so right to be with him.

Tom tightened his hold on Megan and thought how
good it felt to have her here—as if they were meant to
be together. It shouldn't have surprised him that his
mother expected him to propose. But it had. If his
mother had known how viciously Maryanne had rejected him she would understand his hesitation. He
wasn't sure he'd ever trust another woman enough to
open himself to a repeat of that agony.

He recalled the sober advice in *HOW TO MARRY THE WOMAN OF YOUR DREAMS*:

When you feel yourself falling in love with a woman you may be tempted to draw back from the relationship. This fear of commitment is natural because when you admit you're in love it leaves you vulnerable to the pain of rejection. However, if you succumb to the fear of commitment, you'll be robbing yourself of the happiness that comes from marriage to the woman of your dreams.

Loving Megan meant taking risks. If only he had a better idea what she was thinking. Megan hadn't done or said anything to commit herself, either. And he wouldn't be so foolish as to offer his heart again to a woman who didn't want it.

He brought Megan a little closer to his side and pressed a kiss to her temple. More than that and he wouldn't be able to leave her in a few minutes when it was time to go their separate ways to bed. His hand caressed its way up her sleeve, accidentally grazing her breast. He felt her tremble and responded by flicking his thumb gently against the nipple. He felt himself catch fire as her breast tautened beneath his touch. He turned and lay down on the couch, pulling her on top of him, and felt her arch into his swollen manhood. "God, how I've missed you! It seemed more like three months than three weeks."

"I missed you, too." She tensed as one of his hands slipped down between her thighs.

He had to find something to talk about, something to keep his mind off how much he wanted her naked under him. "How was Christmas?"

"The kids loved their presents." She ripped the buttons free on his shirt, and searched out his nipples in the mat of hair on his chest, teasing them with her tongue.

Tom moaned. "You can stop that in about a hundred years."

Megan realized Tom's lips had discovered one of the solitaire diamond earrings she was wearing in her ears. "I love my Christmas present. I was surprised when I opened it." *I hoped you might be thinking of diamonds in another kind of setting.*

She shoved his shirt off his shoulders and admired his skin, which glowed bronze in the light from the fire. "You are so beautiful."

"You're the one who's beautiful." He unzipped her gray-green dress down the back and bared her to his gaze. He reached out and took one nipple into his mouth, feeling it come to life under the lace bra.

Megan's breasts felt full and achy as Tom sucked first one and then the other. She pressed her belly against his arousal, wanting more, needing more, but knowing this was not the time or the place.

"Tom, please . . . Your parents—"

"My parents never come downstairs once they've gone to bed."

"But they might—"

"The General is a creature of habit. They won't bother us. I want you, Megan. I need you."

There was no talk of love from Tom, only *want* and *need*. But she hadn't spoken the words either. She wanted to tell him she loved him, but couldn't. Soon there was no more time to think, as her senses took control. Her fingers entwined in the crisp black hair on Tom's chest, then slipped around to his back and down to his taut buttocks. She arched her body into the male need she could feel hardening against her.

The soft whimpering sound in Megan's throat drove Tom wild. In moments he'd slipped them off the couch onto the carpet and divested them of the rest of their clothes. He craved the delicious feel of his skin against hers. At last they both lay naked before a crackling fire that was nothing compared to the heat burning within them.

He poised himself above her, his thighs pressed against hers, his weight resting on his hands. It would take only a single thrust to bring them together. Yet he paused.

"Megan?"

Megan could see the fierce need in Tom's eyes, and the control that held him rigidly in place. She reached up with her hands and cupped his face, bringing it down for her to kiss. "I want you, Tom. I need you. I love—"

He joined their bodies in one powerful thrust, cutting off her sweet words of love. He tilted her hips with his hands for even deeper penetration. Megan felt the fullness of him and a satisfying oneness, as he began moving in an age-old rhythm. She lifted her legs and bound him to her, releasing him only so that he could thrust again.

His breathing was harsh in her ear and she sought out his lips, his cheeks and chin, and finally his mouth. His tongue mimed the rhythm of lovemaking and Megan sucked on it in an attempt to capture the sensation in the same way she might have captured him inside her if she could. She could feel the spiraling tension, feel her muscles tensing, tightening, feel her heart pounding. She could sense the rising crest of desire in both of them and reached out to meet it. She rode with it, caught on a never-ending wave of ecstasy that tumbled her into a well of dark, deep passion.

Tom's mouth absorbed Megan's cries. She was so intensely giving, so loving, he found himself soaring to heights he'd never reached with another woman. It had taken long minutes before he'd recovered enough to say anything, only to discover that Megan was asleep. He felt a smile form on his face as he looked down at the woman in his arms. He wondered how he'd ever thought he could live without her. Somehow he would have to find the courage to admit his love, and to convince her that they belonged together.

The next morning Megan woke to find herself in bed in the guest room. She was wearing a flimsy nightgown that she had no recollection of donning. She could hardly believe she and Tom had made love in the middle of the living-room floor in his mother's house. She grinned. It had been a crazy thing to do, but was indicative of how crazy she felt about Tom. She wondered if he realized how much she loved him.

"Good morning, sleepyhead."

She automatically pulled the covers up to hide the sheer bodice of her negligee. Two splotches of color grew on her cheeks as she replied, "Good morning."

Tom sat down beside her on the bed and set the breakfast tray he'd brought with him on the end table. When he spoke his voice was husky. "You don't know how hard it was to leave you here alone last night. I wanted to wake up with you in my arms this morning."

"That sounds wonderful. I'd like to see your head on the pillow beside mine."

"Megan, I think we have to talk."

Megan cleared her throat. "About what?"

"Last night you said you loved me."

He tipped her chin up with his hand so her eyes met his. "Did you mean it, or were those just words of passion?"

Megan searched his face, looking for the love she wanted to find. But his expression was carefully blank. She felt vulnerable. She would simply have to trust that his feelings were as strong as her own. "I do love you, Tom. I think I have for a long time. I've just been afraid to say the words."

He exhaled a breath he hadn't known he'd been holding. He took her hands and gently ran his thumb over her knuckles. "I love you, too."

Megan felt her eyes filling with tears and was helpless to stop them when they trickled over.

Tom leaned over and his tongue sipped up the salty drops on her cheeks. "I hope these are tears of happiness."

"Oh, they are! They are!" Megan flung herself into his arms.

His arms circled her, hugging her tight. "Darling, darling Megan, I never thought I'd feel like this again. I want to marry you. I want to be Sarah's and Chris's father. I want us to have children of our own. I—"

Megan jerked herself out of Tom's embrace and scuttled back to the head of the bed, pulling her knees up to her chest and hugging them with her hands.

"Megan? What's wrong? What did I say?"

When Tom started to move toward her, Megan put up a hand to keep him away. "I think you'd better listen to me before you get carried away talking about marriage and children."

Megan watched Tom's features go hard, all the love disappearing as though she'd erased a chalkboard.

His voice was devoid of emotion as he announced, "I'm listening."

"I haven't been totally honest with you."

"Oh?"

Megan tried to meet Tom's gaze, but ended up looking at her toes. "How old do you think I am?"

"What the hell difference does it make?"

Megan looked up at him. "I'm thirty-nine."

"Is that supposed to mean something to me?"

"It means I'm awfully old to be having children, Tom." She took a deep breath. "Before you try and convince yourself or me that I could still have children you have a right to know...I can't.''

Tom was quiet for so long she thought he must not have heard her. "I said I can't have any more children."

"I heard you," he said curtly.

It hurt to hear the pain in his voice. "I had problems when Chris was born and I had an operation. So if you want to marry a woman who can give you more children, you shouldn't marry me."

"Why did you wait until now to tell me this? Were you hoping that I'd demand fertility as a requirement for my wife, so you could claim you didn't qualify?"

Megan was stunned at the fury in Tom's voice. "No! I—"

"Don't worry, Megan. I haven't proposed yet, if that's what's got you so scared. You don't need an excuse to—"

"It isn't an excuse!" she cried, scrambling over to confront him on her knees at the foot of the bed. "How many times did you tell me you wanted a son like you? Or ask me whether I wanted more babies? I can't marry you if children is one of the things you want from me. Because I can't give them to you!"

Megan was off the bed, past Tom and out of the room in an instant. It wasn't until she reached the hall that she realized she had no place to go. She could hear Isabel and the General in the kitchen and she couldn't very well leave the house in her nightgown. She turned around and immediately slammed into Tom's chest.

He captured her by her wrists, and moved with her back into the bedroom, closing the door behind them.

"Dammit, Megan, we have to talk!"

"Let me go!"

"I will when you hear me out."

Megan could tell from the tone of Tom's voice that he wasn't about to change his mind, so she stopped pulling against his strength. The instant she did, he released her wrists and she slumped down onto the bed.

"All right. I'm listening," she said dully.

Tom stood before her, unsure where to start. He said the hardest words first.

"I love you, Megan, but—"

"But that's not enough, is it?" Megan snapped.

Megan found herself yanked up into Tom's embrace, her mouth punished by his. She stiffened against his sensual assault, a sob growing in her throat. She shoved uselessly against his chest with the heels of her hands. She moaned, a helpless, hopeless sound, and felt his mouth immediately soften. He used his lips to plead with her to accept him, not to turn him away. Because she loved him, Megan found herself reaching out to him, returning his love a hundred-fold.

They were bound in each other's arms when Tom's mother opened the door.

"Oh, my. Excuse me. I knocked, but—"

Tom felt his face flush as he abruptly released Megan and stepped back. He was shocked by the puffiness of her lips. It had happened again. That total loss of control where Megan was concerned. It frightened and infuriated him at the same time. He loved her. He wanted her. But what would happen if he married her?

His voice was harsher than he meant it to be when he spoke to Megan. "I'll talk to you later." Then he turned on his heel and left the room.

Megan stared after him, confused by what had just transpired. "Uh...we were just..." She was sure it had been quite clear to Tom's mother what they'd been doing.

"Has he proposed yet?"

Megan's distraught cry brought Isabel across the room to fold the younger woman in her arms. "There, there. It can't be that bad."

"It's awful," Megan said through the tears that fell freely. "I can't marry Tom."

"But whyever not? Surely you know he loves you."

"He says he does. But—"

"No buts. There's nothing to keep you apart."

"Except that I can't have any more children," Megan said bitterly.

Isabel sighed. "So that's what this is all about. How thoughtless of me to have made the remarks I did. If I'd only known...."

"You see why I can't marry Tom."

"I don't see anything of the kind. If I know my son, the fact that you can't have children isn't what has him upset. It's something else. Something that goes back a long way. Something that I blame myself for."

By now Megan's tear-streaked eyes were wide with curiosity.

"Let's sit down a minute, shall we?"

Megan sat down cross-legged on the bed, and to her surprise Isabel shed her shoes and joined her.

"Has Tom told you anything about his childhood?"

"A little."

"Did he tell you about his father?"

"Yes," Megan admitted.

"Then you know how he beat me when he was drunk. He wasn't a bad man, only a weak one. Tom watched his father and vowed that he'd never act like that with a woman. For Tom that meant never letting a woman get too close.

"I was surprised when he married Sally, and sorry when it didn't work out. He told me later that he hadn't been able to let her share his life, that he'd shut her out. He never gave himself permission to let his senses rule, and not his head. After a while, she couldn't take it anymore and left him.

"You're the first woman Tom has brought here to meet me since Sally divorced him. I've been watching you two together. For whatever reason—and reason probably has very little to do with it—Tom has let down his barriers with you. I suspect he loves you more than he's willing to admit, even to himself."

Megan's brow furrowed. "I hadn't realized. If you're right, I've just hurt him very badly. I've got to find him and make things right."

"There'll be time enough for that." Isabel picked up the tray of food that Tom had brought. "This must be ice cold. Why not finish dressing and join me for breakfast?''

Megan managed to meet Isabel's encouraging smile with one of her own. "All right."

Tom wasn't at breakfast. He'd left a message with the General that he had some errands to run. Megan smiled brightly and made conversation at the table even though she was dying inside. Maybe Isabel was wrong. Tom might have let down his barriers for a while, but they were certainly up again, as high and impenetrable as ever.

It was dark by the time Tom returned to his mother's home. He'd spent most of the day at the Alamo. It was dark and cool inside the stone building and with the strong sense of reverence he always felt when he walked inside, he found it a perfect place to think. When he was finished thinking he'd had one more stop to make before returning home. Now he needed to find Megan and share the knowledge he'd acquired.

But Megan was nowhere to be found. He located his mother on the glassed-in porch and demanded, "Where is she?"

"She's gone."

He gave a cry of pain like a wounded animal. "How long ago did she leave?"

"She couldn't get a flight until late. You may still be able to catch her, if that's what you want to do."

Tom turned on his heel to leave but was drawn up short by Isabel's, "Wait!"

"What is it, Mother? I have a plane to catch."

"I'll expect you to bring my new grandchildren to meet me this summer."

Tom grinned. "Count on it!" And then he was gone.

Ten

His Book: "Putting the Ring on Her Finger"

Tom had proposed twice in his lifetime. The first time the woman had said yes, but the marriage had ended in failure. The second time he'd been refused in words so cruel, words that had left such deep scars, that he'd remained single rather than face that kind of pain again. Now he was on his way to ask another woman to become his wife. And he was scared.

He thought Megan loved him enough that she would say yes. But he wasn't positive. The fact that she'd run from him was evidence that they still had problems that needed to be resolved. To calm his doubts he fell back on the safety valve that had gotten him this far. During the entire cab ride to the airport he reviewed the advice on proposing that he'd found in the last chapter of *HOW TO MARRY THE WOMAN OF YOUR DREAMS*.

> *A proposal should be as romantic as you can make it, for this is a moment both of you will remember for the rest of your lives. Tell her you love her, and ask her in simple, honest words to marry you.*
>
> *Acknowledge her objections to marriage if she voices them, but don't let them deter you from your goal: getting her to say yes to your proposal.*

When Tom first saw Megan at the airport he heaved a sigh of relief. He'd been worried that she'd somehow be able to catch an earlier flight. But the instant their eyes met, he knew she was as scared as he was, and that if he didn't act quickly and decisively, they were in danger of losing everything they'd found with one another.

Megan knew running away had never solved anything, but it had seemed the only choice she had. She sincerely believed that until Tom could come to terms with the confession she'd made, it would be far better if they were apart. So when she saw him striding purposefully toward her at the airport, her first inclination was to flee again.

"Don't you dare run from me, Megan Padget!"

Tom's voice wasn't loud, but it was enough to stop Megan in her tracks. She turned and waited for him, her heart in her throat, afraid to hope, but unable to stop herself.

Tom would have liked to wait to propose in an intimate restaurant with champagne and caviar and a candlelit table, but that simply wasn't possible. The middle of a busy airport would have to do. But when he captured Megan's hands and looked deeply into her eyes their surroundings suddenly faded, leaving the two of them alone in the crowd.

"I love you, Megan. I want to spend the rest of my life loving you. Will you marry me?"

"I can't give you any more children," Megan felt compelled to say.

"I know that. Will you marry me?"

"I'll be a demanding wife. I'll want you to share yourself fully with me."

"I know that, too. Will you marry me?"

"I love you, Tom."

"I thought you might, but it's nice to hear you say it. Will you marry me, Megan?"

An irrepressible grin broke out on Megan's face. "Yes, yes, yes, yes! I'll marry you!"

Tom lifted her into his arms and swung her around in a circle, a burst of euphoric laughter breaking the awful tension that had built within him. "God, woman, you've run me a merry chase! But I've caught you now and I'm not about to let you go. Do you still want to go home to Miami?"

"We could be totally alone there," Megan said breathlessly. "The kids will be gone for a few more days. Would you mind?"

"That sounds great to me. We can plan what we're going to say to Sarah and Chris."

They didn't need an airplane, they were both flying so high on happiness, but they had luggage to think of, so they waited for the next plane together. They were delayed by a layover in Atlanta, so when they turned on the lamp in Megan's bedroom it was well past midnight. A feeling of contentment, laced with anticipation, arced between them.

Megan felt unaccountably shy undressing for bed, knowing that Tom was doing the same across the room from her. "This feels strange."

"How so?"

"I don't know. Kind of natural, but new, if you know what I mean."

A wicked grin flashed on Tom's face. "Natural but new. Sounds like something I'd like." He drew on a pair of cotton pajama bottoms that hung low on his hips.

Meanwhile Megan donned the silky nightgown that had been Stephanie's birthday gift to her. It reminded her of the other gift she'd received that day, the one that had brought her to this place, with this man. She felt a rush of love for her children, who in their youthful innocence had wanted her to find this happiness, never realizing the mountains that would have to be climbed in the process.

Megan crossed the room and stepped into Tom's embrace. "If you'd told me on my last birthday that I'd find the right man and be engaged to him before the new year, I'd have laughed in your face," Megan admitted, her lips twisting wryly. "Yet here I am, and here you are, and . . . we are engaged, aren't we?"

Tom chuckled. "It seems in all the excitement I've been a bit remiss. Hold on." He left her and went to rummage in the pocket of his jeans. He came back a moment later and took her left hand in his. "I bought this for you today."

Megan gasped as Tom slid a beautiful sapphire and diamond engagement ring on her finger. She threw her arms around him and gave him a crushing hug. "It's beautiful! You're wonderful! I love you so much!"

After that, although they were both exhausted, they were also too excited to sleep. They opened the bottle of champagne Megan kept in the bottom of the refrigerator in case of a special occasion, and took it with them back into the bedroom. What followed was a night of holding one another, of tender touching and of talking sweet and low. They shared their hopes and dreams, and finally, when it was nearly dawn, they shared their fears.

"I have a question for you," Tom said. "Would you and the kids like to move to Washington?"

Megan had avoided thinking about the issue of where they would live, because she felt sure it was a potential powder keg. But this had been a night for honesty, so she said, "Is there any way you could stay here? I mean, could you still be a political consultant in Miami?"

"Is there a particular reason why you don't want to move?"

"My mom and dad live close by. I love my job. And the children have put down roots. I'm sure we could all adjust if we had to, but to be frank, I'd rather stay here."

Tom's brow furrowed in thought. "It would mean a lot more traveling for me if I lived in Miami. I'd have to be gone from you and the kids at times to do it. But there would be the compensation of being closer to my South American connections.

"Also, I haven't told you because I wasn't sure I wanted to do anything about it, but St. Mark's has offered me a permanent position as chairman of the political science department. I don't see any reason why we can't give living here a try. If things get too difficult we can reassess and see whether it makes sense to move later on."

"I feel like I'm doing all the taking and you're doing all the giving," Megan said.

"Don't kid yourself. We'll both have to make compromises. That's what marriage is all about—two people who love each other learning to bend so that the needs of both are met."

"Are you sure you don't feel cheated when you have to make concessions?" Megan asked. "For instance, will you be sorry later that you married a woman who can't give you more children?"

Megan appreciated the fact that Tom didn't rush to reassure her, that he took the time to formulate what he wanted to say. Because what he said allayed her fears for all time.

"Yes, I'm sorry we won't be able to make a baby together. That would have meant a lot to me. But it would only have been one more blessing added to what we already have. I love Sarah and Chris. I'd like to adopt them, if you—and they—want me to. And I have a son, Todd, that I hardly know. Maybe it's time

I did. That's three children, Megan, more than enough for any man. I'm not so foolish as to yearn for grapes to make wine, when my cup is already full to overflowing."

Two idyllic days followed during which Tom and Megan got out of bed only long enough to eat and regain their energy for another loving free-for-all. It was hard for Megan to kiss Tom goodbye when he finally left the morning her children were supposed to return home. They'd agreed that she should break the news of their engagement to Sarah and Chris, and that he would join them for dinner that evening.

Megan was unbelievably nervous, but told herself it was ridiculous to be worried about how her children would receive the news of her engagement to Tom. After all, they were the ones who'd bought her *YOU DON'T HAVE TO SAY SINGLE*. And they both loved Tom.

She waited until her parents had left before she said, "Can the two of you come into the living room for a minute? I'd like to talk to you."

"What's up, Mom? Is something wrong? It's Tom, isn't it?" Sarah said.

"Nothing's wrong, and Tom will be here for supper." *If the next few minutes go all right.*

Chris sprawled on the sofa. "So why do you want to talk to us?"

"I have an announcement to make." Megan took a deep breath before saying, "Tom and I have decided to get married."

Both Sarah and Chris started talking at once.

"Wait till my friends hear about this! Did he give you a ring? Can I get a new dress for the wedding?"

"Is he going to be our dad now? When are you getting married? Is he going to live here with us?"

"I'll answer all your questions," Megan said, "but first let me make sure that what I'm hearing is that you're both happy about this news."

"Of course I am!" Sarah shouted.

"Yeah! This is great!" Chris echoed.

"So when are you getting married?" Sarah asked.

"We thought we'd have the wedding over spring break and take a short honeymoon then."

Sarah grinned. "That's neat, Mom. I knew that book would do the job. I told Chris so when I saw it in the store."

"I agreed with you, didn't I?" Chris said.

They were still arguing over who was most responsible for her upcoming marriage when Tom arrived for supper that evening. Megan watched Tom's eyes light up when he saw her. When his glance shifted to Sarah and Chris, Megan knew they were experiencing the same warm glow of love.

"I wish you were marrying Mom sooner," Chris told Tom as they were clearing the table after supper.

"Why is that?"

"'Cause if you were my dad maybe you'd take me to the Superbowl."

Tom laughed and ruffled Chris's hair. "There'll be other years. Let's wait until the Dolphins make it and we'll all go. How does that sound?"

"Wow! Mom, did you hear what Tom said?"

Megan smiled at Chris's enthusiasm. It was amazing how a child could condense the parental role so tidily. It wouldn't all be honey and roses, but she felt certain that their love would help them over the rough spots. She realized she was looking forward now to the time when Tom would share the responsibilities and pleasures of being a parent.

As it turned out, the few months until spring break was barely enough time to organize a wedding. Megan felt indebted to her mother and father, to Stephanie and to Irene, for taking much of the burden off her shoulders. Despite their help, or perhaps because of it, she and Tom never had a moment alone. To make matters more complicated, Sarah brought her girlfriends over to gawk at Tom, and Chris brought his friends over so Tom could play football with them. Her time with him was reduced to stolen kisses and snatched embraces. She ached with wanting Tom, and knew it was the same for him.

By the time their wedding day arrived they had both reached a peak of sexual anticipation. It wouldn't have taken much for Megan to step into the nearest empty room with Tom and give free rein to her desires. Fortunately—or unfortunately—she never found Tom and a free room in the house at the same time.

They held the wedding in the backyard, where the bougainvillea draped the arbor that covered the outdoor patio. The gardenia bushes Megan had planted when she'd first moved into the house were full of blossoms, the aroma of which permeated the whole backyard. There were only a few of Megan's and Tom's closest friends present, along with both sets of parents, Megan's children and Irene and Randy. Still, Megan was very much aware of being in the limelight. When the minister asked, "Do you take this man to be your lawfully wedded husband?" she had to swallow over a lump in her throat before she could say, "I do."

She heard Tom's solemn response, but the rest of the wedding was a blur, as was the reception. Nor was she much aware of the flight to Key West where they had made reservations to stay at a quaint guest house. In fact, it wasn't until Tom closed the door of their room and they were utterly, completely alone that the fog lifted and Megan realized where she was and what she'd done.

"We're married."

"That's the usual result of a wedding," Tom replied, his lips quirking. "Are you all right, Megan? You seem a little—"

"Spaced out?" Megan offered with a rueful smile. "That's because I can't believe all this is real. I feel like I've been in limbo the past few months. It's hard to believe we're finally alone together...."

It was as though speaking that truth crystallized the need that had grown between them over the past months. Tom took a step closer, then stopped. His glance slid to the bed, to the comfortable, overstuffed chair in the corner, to the lushly carpeted floor and then back to Megan.

"Where would you like to make love for the first time as man and wife?"

She looked up at him from under lowered lashes. "In the shower." She blushed as his brows rose in surprise. "It's always been a fantasy of mine, if you want to know the truth."

When she started to pull off the cotton shirt she'd traveled in, he reached out a hand and stopped her. Slowly, sensually, he unfastened the line of buttons at her throat until he'd revealed the shadow between her breasts. He nudged the shirt open with his fingers, then leaned over to press a line of kisses along her shoulder and down across her breastbone. When he could no longer stand the torment of touching without seeing, his hands gripped the bottom of the shirt and easily drew it over her head, leaving Megan temptingly dressed in the laciest bra she owned.

She waited for him to remove his own shirt, but instead he took her hands and brought them to his chest. "Would you mind returning the favor?"

"My pleasure," she said, a shy smile curving her lips. Megan indulged herself by taking her time releasing his buttons, then threading her fingers through the crisp hair on his chest, finding his nipples and playing with them until he gasped. She laid her cheek against his chest and listened to the thundering beating of his heart. When she finally slipped the shirt off his shoulders she could feel him trembling with need.

He reached over to undo the front clasp on her bra and removed it. Then he drew her close. She sighed with pleasure at the feel of her breasts nestled against the wiry hair on his chest.

"God, Megan, you feel so good! I want my skin against yours everywhere." His hands fumbled with the catch on her skirt and Megan helped him undo it. The next few moments were frenzied as they divested themselves of their clothes. When they finally stood naked before one another, Megan took Tom's hand and led him into the sea green-and-peach-tiled bathroom.

She started to step into the tub, but Tom's hand delayed her. "Let me adjust the water for us first. How would you like it? Hot? Lukewarm?"

"How about a little on the cool side?" Megan suggested.

Tom grinned at her. "I'm afraid that's not going to do much to dampen my ardor."

Megan's glance skipped down and she could see what he meant. "I just thought...we'll get so warm...."

Tom laughed. "You're absolutely right, of course. Come on, step in. I think the temperature's right now."

He took her elbow to support her as she stepped into the tub. He followed behind her and stood facing her, his body shimmering as the water sluiced off him. He unwrapped a bar of soap and began making a rich lather in his hands. "Any places you'd like me to pay special attention to?"

Megan felt flushed with excitement. It was difficult to speak frankly, but she was determined to do so. "My throat. My breasts. My stomach. The small of my back. And...anything else that catches your fancy."

Tom's eyes were hooded, his body tense as he gently wrapped his arms around her and placed his thumbs on the dimples just above her buttocks. "Here?"

Megan's arms went around Tom's neck. She closed her eyes and swayed toward him. "Uh huh."

While the shower pulsed down on them, he massaged the small of her back with his thumbs, working out the knots that had formed during the long day.

Megan felt deliciously languorous by the time Tom gripped her around the waist with one of his hands and brought the other up to caress her neck. His thumb found the rapidly beating pulse in her throat and he leaned down to whisper in her ear, "You're so beautiful, Megan. I love the feel of your body under my hands. Sleek and soft. Warm and wet and willing. I want you."

Megan trembled from the sheer eroticism of his words. When his hand slipped down to her breast, she arched her back, and felt her nipple hardening in the palm of his hand.

"Please," she murmured.

"What do you want, sweetheart? Tell me. I only want to please you."

"Would you . . . touch me with your mouth?"

She felt his body shudder as he gathered her to him, cupping her breast and pressing it upward with his hand at the same time his mouth came down to possess her. He bit down on the nipple, causing a pleasurable pain that he immediately soothed with his tongue. Then he sucked her breast into his mouth, causing a spasm of desire to shudder through her.

Megan's fingernails dug into Tom's shoulders, and her mouth found the lobe of his ear, biting and licking in the same way he was caressing her breast.

His hand slid down her belly, across to her hip-bones and beyond to the curls sheltering her femininity. When he found her bud of desire with his thumb, she flowered for him.

She wanted to give, but she was caught in a vortex of taking. She clung to Tom, mindlessly seeking out whatever part of him she could touch with her mouth and hands. His shoulders, his chest, his hips, his buttocks, at last caressing that part of him that was stiff and ready for her.

Breathlessly she pleaded with him. "Tom... Tom... please... I want you."

His mouth found hers in a kiss that sent both of them reeling. He turned their bodies so he was leaning against the tile wall for a moment, long enough to warm it for her, and then he turned them again so that she was pressed against the smooth surface. She felt the muscles in his back and shoulders bunch as he lifted her easily. A moment later he was deep inside her and her legs were wrapped around his hips. He pressed her hard against the wall, moving himself deeper, tilting her hips, needing more, taking more... and giving more.

Megan responded in an ecstatic frenzy, arching, holding him when he sought to leave her, demanding that he take from her, that he give to her, that they slake the need born of their love for one another.

"My God, Megan. You feel so good. I don't think I can wait—"

"Tom... I can't either...."

In the moment of extremity they both cried out, harsh, painful sounds that had nothing to do with pain, but everything to do with the wonder of the heaven they'd created on earth.

Megan was panting hard, sucking air to relieve her tortured lungs, and so was Tom. He slowly eased her legs down and held her until he was sure she could stand on her own. Even then he was reluctant to free her from his embrace. He took her with him as he stepped back into the strongest part of the shower spray.

They let the water pour over them, cooling the steamy heat that rose from their feverish bodies.

Tom finally reached over and shut off the water. He wrapped Megan in a fluffy towel and found another one for himself. Then he lifted her up and carried her into the bedroom. He pulled the covers down and laid her on the clean, white sheets before joining her there. He held her close in his arms, not wanting to sleep, but feeling an inevitable drowsiness.

"Megan," he murmured, already half asleep.

"What, Tom?"

"Do you think if we practice that we can get it perfect?"

Megan smiled to herself. "I'm willing to give it a try if you are."

"It's going to be wonderful, Megan. I promise you that."

"We'll be one of those couples who lives happily ever after. You just wait and see if we aren't," Megan concurred, as her eyes drooped closed.

They drifted off to sleep, certain of their love for one another and of their willingness to make their marriage work. They were blissfully unaware that each of them had received a wedding gift designed to make their pronouncements come true.

For in Tom's suitcase was his present from Randy and Irene—a book called *HOW TO MAKE YOUR MARRIAGE LAST.*

And in Megan's suitcase was her present from Sarah and Chris—a book called *ONE HUNDRED WAYS TO KEEP THE ROMANCE IN YOUR MARRIAGE.*

* * * * *

Silhouette Classics

COMING IN APRIL...

THORNE'S WAY by Joan Hohl

When *Thorne's Way* first burst upon the romance scene in 1982, readers couldn't help but fall in love with Jonas Thorne, a man of bewildering arrogance and stunning tenderness. This book quickly became one of Silhouette's most sought-after early titles.

Now, Silhouette Classics is pleased to present the reissue of *Thorne's Way*. Even if you read this book years ago, its depth of emotion and passion will stir your heart again and again.

And that's not all!

Silhouette Special Edition

COMING IN JULY...

THORNE'S WIFE by Joan Hohl

We're pleased to announce a truly unique event at Silhouette. Jonas Thorne is back, in *Thorne's Wife*, a sequel that will sweep you off your feet! Jonas and Valerie's story continues as life—and love—reach heights never before dreamed of.

Experience both these timeless classics—one from Silhouette Classics and one from Silhouette Special Edition—as master storyteller Joan Hohl weaves two passionate, dramatic tales of everlasting love!

You'll flip . . . your pages won't!
Read paperbacks *hands-free* with

Book Mate · I

The perfect "mate" for all your romance paperbacks

Traveling • Vacationing • At Work • In Bed • Studying • Cooking • Eating

Perfect size for all standard paperbacks, this wonderful invention makes reading a pure pleasure! Ingenious design holds paperback books OPEN and FLAT so even wind can't ruffle pages – leaves your hands free to do other things. Reinforced, wipe-clean vinyl-covered holder flexes to let you turn pages without undoing the strap . . . supports paperbacks so well, they have the strength of hardcovers!

Pages turn WITHOUT opening the strap.

SEE-THROUGH STRAP

Reinforced back stays flat.

Built in bookmark

BOOK MARK

BACK COVER HOLDING STRIP

10˝ x 7¼˝, opened.
Snaps closed for easy carrying, too.

Available now. Send your name, address, and zip code, along with a check or money order for just $5.95 + .75¢ for postage & handling (for a total of $6.70) payable to Reader Service to:

Reader Service
Bookmate Offer
901 Fuhrmann Blvd.
P.O. Box 1396
Buffalo, N.Y. 14269-1396

Offer not available in Canada
*New York and Iowa residents add appropriate sales tax.

BM-G

Silhouette Special Edition®

NAVY BLUES
Debbie Macomber

Between the devil and the deep blue sea...

At Christmastime, Lieutenant Commander Steve Kyle finds his heart anchored by the past, so he vows to give his ex-wife wide berth. But Carol Kyle is quaffing milk and knitting tiny pastel blankets with a vengeance. She's determined to have a baby, and only one man will do as father-to-be—the only man she's ever loved...her own bullheaded ex-husband!

You met Steve and Carol in NAVY WIFE (Special Edition #494)—you'll cheer for them in NAVY BLUES (Special Edition #518). (And as a bonus for NAVY WIFE fans, newlyweds Rush and Lindy Callaghan reveal a surprise of their own....)

Each book stands alone—together they're Debbie Macomber's most delightful duo to date! Don't miss

NAVY BLUES
Available in April,
only in *Silhouette Special Edition*.
Having the "blues" was never
so much fun!
